# EARTH SPELLS ARE EASY

*Grimoires of a Middle-aged Witch Book One*

RENEE GEORGE

Barkside of the Moon Press

Earth Spells Are Easy

Grimoires of a Middle-aged Witch Book 1



Print: May 2021

ISBN: 978-1-947177-39-0

Publisher: Barkside of the Moon Press

## PRAISE FOR RENEE GEORGE

"Sense and Scent Ability by Renee George is a delightfully funny, smart, full of excitement, up-all-night fantastic read! I couldn't put it down. The latest installment in the Paranormal Women's Fiction movement, knocks it out of the park. Do yourself a favor and grab a copy today!"

— —ROBYN PETERMAN NYT BESTSELLING AUTHOR

"I'm loving the Paranormal Women's Fiction genre! Renee George's humor shines when a woman of a certain age sniffs out the bad guy and saves her bestie. Funny, strong female friendships rule!"

— -- MICHELLE M. PILLOW, NYT & USAT BESTSELLING AUTHOR

"I smell a winner with Renee George's new book, Sense & Scent Ability! The heroine proves that being over fifty doesn't have to stink, even if her psychic visions do."

— -- MANDY M. ROTH, NY TIMES BESTSELLING AUTHOR

"Sense & Scent Ability is everything! Nora Black is sassy, smart, and her smell-o-vision is scent-sational. I can't wait for the next Nora book!

— —MICHELE FREEMAN, *AUTHOR OF HOMETOWN HOMICIDE, A SHERIFF BLUE HAYES MYSTERY*

**As a forty-three-year-old, newly divorced, single mom, I know two things for certain, starting over sucks, and magic isn't real. At least that's what I thought. I mean, starting over really does stink, but when it comes to magic, I have to rethink everything.**

I've spent the last year since my ex left me going through the motions. Get up. Work. Care for a grumpy teenager. Cook dinner. Go to bed. Wash. Rinse. Repeat.

Nothing changes... Until it does.

After bidding on a box of old books at an estate auction, I'm experiencing changes.

And I'm not talking about menopause.

My garden gnome Linda has come to life. No, really. Her name is Linda, and she never shuts up. A chonky cat with a few secrets of his own has adopted me. And a gorgeous professor of the occult tells me I'm a witch.

Right now, I'm not sure who's crazier—me, Linda or the hottie professor.

If this is my new reality, it's nature's cruel midlife trick. I'm learning fast that earth spells might be easy, but they aren't cheap. All magic exacts a toll, and if I don't master the elements, the elements will be the death of me.

Literally.

*For my son, Taylor, who takes great pleasure in scaring the crap out of me whenever possible. Watching you grow up is a great pleasure, and I'm so proud of the man you've become!*

## ACKNOWLEDGMENTS

I have to thank sooo many people for this book!

First, Robyn Peterman, Michele Freeman, and Robbin Clubb, my critique partners, who know just when to kick my ass when I need it! Thank you, Lindas! (You all will get this when you read the story, LOL).

Second, to my brood of siblings and my son for being inspirations in this story. If moments feel real, it's because I have some awesome experiences to pull from in my life.

Third, to the readers and my Rebels, without you all, what would be the point? I am so happy and blessed to have you guys in my corner!

Forth, but not least, coffee. Thank you strong black coffee, for always being there for me in my time of need. You are the miracle in my life.

# CHAPTER 1

THE GARLICKY SCENT OF TAKE-OUT CREATED A nauseating stench I found hard to ignore. Now, I would forever associate Mongolian Beef with divorce, and it made me want to yark.

I passed the legal documents across the kitchen table to my lawyer Donald Overton III then glanced around my kitchen. "Sorry about the mess, Don." There were two plates, silverware, and cups in the sink, and it had been the third time I'd said I was sorry since his arrival.

"The place is cleaner than my house," he said.

Don, who was a six-foot-four man with rounded shoulders and a big, balding head to match, wasn't just my lawyer. He was also my brother-in-law. Which meant I knew he was stretching the truth to spare my feelings. My sister Rose was a meticulous housekeeper. "Is that it?" I asked.

He gave me a sympathetic look, emphasis on the *pathetic*, and nodded. "That's it, Iris. Done is done."

I rubbed my face. "Done is done," I repeated. "I'm officially Iris Everlee." I'd legally changed it a few weeks earlier. Still, it hadn't felt definitive that I was no longer a Callahan until I'd signed the divorce papers.

I'd wasted eighteen years married to a man who left me for someone else. Someone younger. Someone male. My ex, it turned out, was bisexual. I have always been open-minded. I genuinely believe, love is love and that people should live their truths. But when it's your husband, it's a lot harder to be congratulatory about someone discovering their "authentic self."

"Thanks for bringing those to me." I stood up from the table. "I have to get Michael up for practice."

Michael was my seventeen-year-old son. I worried he'd suffered the most during the divorce. But my son had always been a quiet child, not distant or anti-social, just even keel and low drama. It made it extremely difficult to gauge his real feelings most of the time.

"Is he still playing football?" Don asked.

"Yep. Today's the first day of spring training."

Don added, "You look like you need a friend. You should call Rose."

Unable to shake the feeling of trepidation, I said, "I'm fine. I'll be okay."

Don gave me a grim smile, then gathered up the paperwork and slipped it into a folder. "I'll get these filed at the courthouse today. You and Michael should come to dinner tomorrow night."

I stood up and walked him out of the kitchen and through the living room to the front door. "I'll call Rose later. I promise," I told him, which had been the only promise Don had been trying to extract. Of course, I hadn't promised *when* I would call.

"Please do. You know how Rose gets." My brother-in-law gave me a gentle shoulder squeeze, then left.

I had three sisters and one brother. Rose, the youngest of us all, had taken on the responsibility as the family worry-wart since our mother died of pancreatic cancer five years earlier. The doctors had given her three or four months to live, but she'd died three weeks later in her sleep because the cancer had strangled her aorta and caused an aneurysm.

I closed the door and made my way down the dark hallway past the kitchen. Even with the door closed, the foul scents of boy stink threatened to knock me off my feet. Garlic leftovers had nothing on *Ewwww de Son*. I tapped on the door. No response. I pounded my fist against the wood. Still no response.

I opened the door a crack. "Hello?" I leaned on the door to open it wider as the sickly sweet and sour odors hit me full force, burning the back of my nostrils.

My eyesight adjusted to the dark. I saw a small mountain of dirty clothes wedged behind the door, barring further entry. I could see long toes peeking over the edge of a queen-sized mattress. Otherwise, I wouldn't have known a human being occupied the bed.

"Michael, damn it." Lately, "damn it" had been his middle name. "Let me in."

"What do you want?" came his muffled voice full of sleepy annoyance.

"I want you to open this stupid door right now."

"Go away."

"I'll go away. I'll go away to the garage and get a screwdriver and a hammer and take this freaking door off its hinges." Screw this. I pushed the door as hard as I could. Mount Dirt & Grime slid across the carpet and allowed me entry.

His foot drifted out of sight. He was moving—another good sign.

"What the hell died in your room? It smells like a serial killer's drop zone."

The boy sat up, his short hair looking too perfect to be slept in, just like his father. He scratched his patchy goatee. "Dramatic much?" His voice, low and pleasant in tone, held an edge of sarcasm.

I fought back a smile. My kid was beautiful, no doubt about it. He was one of the few things Evan and I had done right.

He blinked his soft brown eyes in my direction. "I'm not going to practice."

"Oh, you're going." I picked up a pair of sweatpants, a green pair at the top of the pile, and chucked them at him. "Get dressed."

He groaned and threw himself onto the bed, pulling the covers over his shoulders. "I'm tired."

"You wouldn't be so tired if you weren't up all night playing video games with your buddies."

He grunted. Translation: *Whatever.*

"Michael Evan Callahan, you will get yourself out of bed this minute. You promised your father."

He moaned his dissent. "Coach is going to be there," he replied.

"If you want a relationship with your dad, you're going to have to come to terms with the fact that Coach Adam is a part of his life now." I sounded so reasonable, even to my own ears. Inside, I was screaming. It had been a year since Evan and I had separated, and most of the time, I tried to not hate him for what he'd done to our family, but sometimes I struggled with taking the higher road.

"Yeah, well, you didn't catch them going at it." He was sitting up now, rubbing the sleep from his eyes. "And you expect me to come to terms with it."

Unfortunately, my son had discovered his father's infidelity before me. He'd gone to talk to Coach Adam after school hours and found him and Evan kissing in the coach's office. Michael had come home and locked himself in his bedroom that night. I could still see his hurt and rage. Being caught by our kid was what prompted Evan to finally come clean with me.

Sighing, I sat on the bed next to Michael and put my hand on his shoulder. "Kissing is not going at it," I said.

My oldest sister Dahlia was a family counselor. She'd recommended someone for the family to see, including Evan, in order for us to move forward with our lives.

"Close enough," he countered.

It took months for Michael to even look at his father, then a few months more for him to have a civil conversation with him. I was angry with Evan, but still, I was glad that Michael was finally seeing him again. They'd been taking it slowly. A few lunches and dinners here and there. One month ago, their relationship had taken another setback when Evan and Adam decided to go public and move in together.

I missed the days when I could scoop Michael into my arms and cuddle him. He was at that age now where he would have pulled away if I tried to comfort him. As it was, I could feel him shrink at my consoling touch. How could I expect him to understand and accept his father's new life when I could hardly think about him without my own rage clouding my mind? I felt like I'd wasted my best years on him. He'd promised to love me until *death do we part.* Yes, I lost my husband, but I'd also lost my best friend. Evan and I had more in common than anyone I'd ever met. We had the same tastes in books, music, and movies. We'd shared similar political and philosophical beliefs, and we'd rarely ran out of conversation.

On top of that, our sex life had been good. Don't get me wrong, we'd had our share of arguments. It's hard to be with someone for eighteen years and not have any fights, but we'd always made up. In other words, his falling in love with someone else, regardless of gender, had been a complete blindside.

"Michael," I said, my voice gentle but strained. "I understand that you're uncomfortable around your dad and Adam but avoiding them is not going to make your life any better or easier. Do you want a relationship with your father?"

The teenager raised a wary brow. "Don't shrink me, Mom. That's what you pay Dr. Bradford for."

I narrowed my gaze. "Well, do you? Do you want a relationship with your father? And keep in mind, he's the only father you have." I wasn't above deploying mommy-guilt. "Your dad changed your diapers, coached your baseball and basketball teams. He attended every sporting event you ever played in high school. And he loves you," I said with as much gentleness as I could manage. "Now tell me, do you want a relationship with your father? Yes or no?"

"Sure," he said more than a little grudgingly. "But not with Coach."

"I'm not trying to make you have a relationship with Adam, but he and your father are a package right now." The words, even from my own lips, were a punch in the gut. Evan was a package with someone else now, and like Michael, I had to find a way to come to terms with it.

My teenaged son grunted. Unsympathetically, I clapped my hands to get his attention. "Get. Up."

"I hate you," he said through gritted teeth as he clambered from the bed.

I tried not to let the hurt show on my face. There were plenty of times I'd thought the same words to my mother when I was a teenager, but I never meant it, and I reminded myself as I let out a slow breath that Michael didn't mean it either. "You can hate me all you want, son, just as long as you mind me."

After dressing, and before he left the house, Michael gave me a rare hug and mumbled "love you" in my ear.

"I know," I said. "Love you more." And out the door he went. Once I was alone, my breath started coming faster, harder, and my pulse kicked up a notch—a feeling I knew all too well. This was the beginning of a panic attack. I tried to slow my exhales through pursed lips. *Blow out the candle*, I told myself, as I raced for the back door.

I quickly shoved it open and staggered into my floral paradise, aka my backyard garden. It was a brilliant mixture of colorful wildflowers and herbs. *Cleome and zinnias to attract butterflies and hummingbirds*, my mother had said when she'd help me plan the garden. There were yarrow plants for ladybugs. And fennel and dill, which are supposed to attract beneficial insects, but frankly, after all these years, I couldn't remember which bugs were good. I'd turned the fountain on in the spring, and the sound of trickling water started to soothe my anxiety.

I sat on a bench near a patch of garden phlox. The plants were all green now, but in July, delicate, pale-pink flowers would cluster in bunches. I put my elbows on my knees and lowered my head.

Linda stared at me with contempt. I flipped her off. She didn't react. Of course, she wouldn't. Linda was a stone garden gnome. I'd turned her around the night before, so she was staring at the dill and not at the bench. But—I was guessing—Michael had moved her to mess with me. The kid loved freaking me out. It was his new favorite game of let's see how many ways we can startle Mom.

Her beady eyes always creeped me out. More than once, I'd contemplated tossing her out, but she'd been a gift from my mother.

*Every garden needs a gnome*, she'd told me. *And this sweet girl will keep your garden lush*. Like a mini-Santa, the gnome had a snow-white beard. Mom had painted its hat and tunic pink.

"How do you know it's female?" I'd asked my mother.

"Oh." She'd given me a knowing look. "She's full of feminine energy." My mother had tapped her chest. "I can feel it in here."

I could've done without a gnome, but Mom loving the ugly statuette had softened my feelings toward the little creature.

"What now?" I asked Linda. "What do I do with my life now?"

I waited for a few seconds for a response I knew would

never come. A rustle in the bushes drew my attention away from my stone nemesis. Two long ears twitched above a small rosemary bush, followed by the rest of the rabbit. It was much larger than an Eastern cottontail and smaller than a desert jackrabbit. I'd seen it several times since the beginning of spring, and I wondered what in my garden kept the little fella coming back.

I stood up and narrowed my gaze on my recurrent garden guest. "Hello, Bunny Foo-foo?"

The rabbit, reddish-brown in color, twitched its nose at me. The hair on my head and my arms raised as if the air had turned staticky around me. Only, there was hardly any breeze this morning. The rabbit scurried back behind some bushes, and by the time I walked over, I saw a burrowed-out spot under my privacy fence. The electric tingle I'd felt had disappeared with the small bushy-tailed beast.

I began to look up types of hares on my phone when it rang, saving me from going down that proverbial and literal rabbit hole. I smiled as the name of the caller flashed on my screen. It was my second to oldest sister, Marigold.

"Hey, sis," I answered. "What's up?"

"What are you doing tomorrow night?" she asked. No, how are you? No, sorry about your divorce. I loved that about my hippy-dippy sister. She knew how to avoid a sore subject.

I grinned. "I'm watching *Hospital Blues*. It's a new episode."

She sighed. "That's what DVRs are for. You can record it. Is there anything you can't get out of?"

I made a mental calculation of all the things I had to do this week, including anything involving work or Michael, and couldn't think of a darn thing. He was old enough now to drive himself to practices, and I'd finished editing "Don't Let Your Participle Dangle," a follow-up textbook to "Where Did I Misplace My Modifier?"

I used to be a professor of English out at Darling University, located just outside my hometown of Southill Village in the Ozark Mountains in Northern Arkansas near the Missouri border. I quit when Michael was born and had been working from home, living the glamorous life of a textbook editor ever since.

Unfortunately, I wouldn't have my next assignment until June tenth, so I didn't have a reason to say no to Marigold. "Is washing my hair a good excuse?"

Her tone was bright. "Not even in the slightest. Dress casual," she said. "I'll pick you up at four-thirty."

"So early? What are we doing?"

"There's an estate auction going on in New Weston. We are going to bid on something eccentric and fun."

"We're going to do what?" I grabbed my coffee from the counter and sat down at my dining room table. "

"Going to an estate auction. Ruth Boothwell died three months ago without any heirs, and her estate is auctioning off loads of fancy stuff."

"Fancy stuff, huh?" I asked skeptically. "Look, Mar. I don't have time to go to an estate auction."

"Come on, Iris. What else have you got planned?"

"Washing my hair. Shaving my legs. Waxing my mustache."

Marigold laughed. "It's about time. Self-care is the first step in reclaiming your life. But you can do that tonight. Besides, this is more than just a leisure trip. A colleague of mine, Professor Keir Quinn, has written a book and needs a good editor before he starts submitting it to publishers."

Marigold taught Women's Studies at Darling U. She, like me, had gone the academia route. This wasn't the first time she'd asked me if I would look at a "friend's" manuscript. The last one she'd asked me to look at had been a romantic thriller set in South Florida. I'd given it a hard pass.

"I don't know how many times I have to tell you that I don't do fiction, but...I don't do fiction."

Of course, I read fiction for pleasure, but I didn't want to have to ponder if a comma should exist in a sentence or if it was a choice the writer made to leave it out. Same with sentence fragments and other style issues that might or might not be on purpose. I liked the grammatical and mechanical clarity in which textbooks were written.

"I know you don't do fiction," Marigold shot back. "So, it's a good thing Keir's writing is of the non-fiction variety."

"Mills & Laden Academic Press sends me plenty of work to keep me busy."

She sucked her teeth, producing a sound of sheer annoyance. "I know you only get one book a month, and I also happen to know that you are amazingly fast at your job. Besides, you could use extra money right now, right? And this guy is willing to pay double your normal fees."

I sat down and closed my eyes as I prayed for patience, then asked, "Why would he do that?"

"Because Keir needs it done fast. You know how it is at universities. Publish or perish. Besides, it's an easy gig." My sister sounded exasperated with me. "You should take it."

"It's only easy if he's a half-decent writer."

"He is," Marigold assured me. "Look, come with me to

the auction. Talk to the man. And if you decide to turn down the job, no harm, no foul."

The divorce, even with the sister-in-law lawyer discount, had been costly. I wondered if Rose had reached out to Marigold, and the two of them had cooked up this scheme to help me financially. I did need the money. And aside from that, even if I decided not to take the gig, going to an estate auction might be fun. The idea of getting out and doing something that wasn't work, kid, or husband—I shook my head at my mental slip—ex-husband—related stirred excitement in me.

"Fine," I finally said. "What time should I pick you up tomorrow?"

"I can drive," she protested.

"Barely," I told her. "Do you want me to go or not?"

I heard her harrumph. "I'll come over to your house at four, but you can drive," she said before I could protest. "The auction starts at five-thirty, but I want to get there early enough to check out the sale items."

"I'll be ready with bells on."

"Excellent," she said. "And Iris..."

"Yeah?"

"You know if you want to talk...about today or whatever, I'm here for you."

I nodded even though she couldn't see me. "I do know. Love you, sis."

"Love you back."

# CHAPTER 2

I'D CHANGED MY JEANS THREE TIMES. NOTHING SEEMED TO fit right anymore. According to the digital scale in the bathroom, I'd gained ten pounds in the past three months. I hadn't noticed until my pants had become uncomfortably tight. Unfortunately, I couldn't hide the muffin top pants created with my stomach unless I wore loose, and in my eyes, unflattering shirts. Resolved to my fate, I'd put on a pair of yoga pants and a flowing top.

"I told you to dress casual," Marigold said as she got into the car.

"This is casual," I replied.

"I meant fancy auction casual, not binge-watching past seasons of The Great British Bake-Off casual."

"I can go like this, or I can stay home," I said as I pulled out of the driveway and headed out of the neighborhood.

"Fine." Her lower lip jutted in a pouty sulk. "This will have to do."

My sister, who was five-eight, two inches taller than me,

and thin as a reed—unlike me—wore wide-leg jeans and a Boho-chic tunic top with a light blue and yellow floral print that flattered her black hair and tan skin. We looked nothing alike, but of course, we wouldn't. I, like the rest of my siblings, had been adopted when I was young. One thing I learned at an early age was that blood didn't make you family. Love, support, and devotion created family. I had all three in spades with my siblings.

Marigold took a bottle of perfume from her satchel purse and gave herself a spritz. I smiled as the floral notes of Chanel No. 5 filled the car. It had been Marigold's favorite since high school. She'd bought herself a bottle with babysitting money when she was sixteen. It had made her feel grown-up and very French. *Ooo-la-la.*

I took the highway exit. As we drove out of Southill Village, Marigold grew unusually quiet.

"What is it?" I asked.

My sister frowned. "You know you're an attractive woman, right?"

I snorted. "What's your point?"

"My friend, the guy with the book, he's seriously handsome. Like, super-hot. And I just thought..."

I held up my hand. "Stop right there. I have no interest in being set up."

"Okay." Marigold leaned forward and rubbed her knees. "I won't set you up."

I raised a brow at her. "Did you already set me up?"

"No," she denied. When I gave her a pithy glare, she shook her head. "Honest. I didn't do any matchmaking beyond getting you in the same place as him. And he does have a book that he's interested in having you edit."

"What's this book about?"

"Something about alchemy and symbols of the occult, I think."

"What does he teach? Defense Against the Dark Arts?"

"Harry Potter called and told you to shut up." She rolled her eyes at me and sucked her teeth. "Professor Quinn teaches classes on occult religions."

"Soooo...it *is* Defense Against the Dark Arts."

Marigold snickered. "Doctor Regan nearly swallowed his false teeth when the university hired Professor Quinn."

Doctor Phillip Regan was the chair of the Religious Studies Department. It was in the same building as the English department when I'd been an instructor there eighteen years ago. He was old then. "Regan has to be a hundred years old. I can't believe he hasn't retired yet."

"He just turned eighty-eight, but the pious bastard keeps on ticking. I'm pretty sure he crosses himself daily when he passes Professor Quinn's office."

I giggled. "Does Regan carry holy water and a wooden cross as well?"

"I don't think that works on pagans," Marigold pointed out with a grin.

"Okay, so tell me why a professor of the paranormal is interested in an estate auction? Is the house haunted?"

Marigold smiled. "Apparently, Old Lady Boothwell has a lot of weird stuff she's collected over the years, and the auction house hired him to authenticate some of the items."

"So, she was into all the hoodoo hokum."

"Something like that," she said.

"And your friend is too?"

"Well, he does teach Hokum One-Oh-One," she snickered

"Har har." Marigold had been teaching Women's Studies at the university for over ten years, and I'd never heard her talk about this professor of the occult. "Is that even a discipline?"

"What? Hokum?"

I shook my head and smirked. "Yes, hokum. How does someone get a degree in the occult?"

"I don't really know," Marigold said. "But I'm sure there's a degree program out there somewhere. You can major in just about anything these days." She shrugged. "This is Keir's first semester at Darling."

The way she said his name denoted a fondness that went beyond friendship. "Just how well do you know this professor?"

"It's nothing like that," my sister assured me. "Keir and I are strictly friends. No benefits. Give him a chance, okay? I know you're going to adore him."

"I'm sure I won't." The air conditioner blasted frigid air against my chest. I reached out and closed the vent, then put on my blinker and turned down Boothwell Manor Road, so named for the manor built at the end of the drive. "Where did this professor of paranormal live before he moved to our neck of the woods?"

"He spent a few years in Ireland for his doctorate. But I think he comes from one of the coasts."

I laughed. "That really narrows it down. So, Quinn is either from California, New York, or Texas?"

"You forgot Alaska," Marigold smirked. "Probably not

Texas. I think he's from the east somewhere, but I won't swear to it."

There were multiple rows of cars and trucks lining the long driveway leading up to the main house. I had to stomp the brakes once to avoid hitting a woman who had just willy-nilly walked in front of my car.

My sister reached over and laid on my horn for a moment, but the woman walking in front of us didn't even look up. "Cripes, what is wrong with these people?"

"Distracted with dreams of hitting it big on the Antiques Roadshow." My father loved both the British and the American versions of the show. He had many of them recorded to VCR cassettes and stacked like books in his living room bookshelves.

"Does Dad's VCR still work?"

Marigold frowned at me. "I think so. Why?"

"Just thinking about all those hours of recorded shows from PBS."

Marigold laughed. "Like Bob Ross and Hee Haw."

I grinned and shook my head. "Among others."

I parked on a tuft of grass between two trees, thankful for a compact car. Otherwise, we'd have been walking a half-mile up to the palatial house. After, we headed up the road with everyone else.

"I can't believe how many people are here." I'd been to a few estate auctions in the past, but I'd never seen one quite so well attended. Probably because estates this lavish usually got hauled off to real auction houses.

"Everybody is curious about all the stuff Old Lady Boothwell left behind," Marigold said. "She was a bit of a recluse at the end, but rumor has it she was still collecting weird shit up until her last days."

"Who doesn't love weird shit?"

"Right?" Marigold said with excitement. "This is going to be awesome."

Her enthusiasm was contagious. I felt giddy as we took the steps up to the expansive and open front door. Of course, by the time we'd signed in and got our bidding numbers, we were shoulder to shoulder with the crowd, and the shine of this adventure had tarnished. Sardines weren't packed this tight.

"Is it too late to go home?" I asked. I was still a bit of a raw nerve after signing divorce papers, and I was beginning to think that maybe this wasn't the distraction I needed. "We could eat our weight in ice cream and binge-watch cozy mysteries on that British channel that you love."

Marigold turned her gaze on me. "Tempting, but no. We're here, so let's do it."

The items for the auction were set out on tables with tags, and the rumors about the late Mrs. Boothwell's eccentric taste had not been exaggerated. She had a Victorian palmistry sculpture, a wand made of purple heartwood, and some ceremonial masks from Africa, Japan, Mexico, and the Bahamas. A display shelf housed twenty fertility statuettes. Half were female depictions with large breasts and rounded bellies. The other half were of the male variety with giant phalluses, pointing toward the crowd of eager buyers.

One had a tall headdress that was skinnier than his erection. I leaned in for a closer look at the tag. Like it had in my garden the day before, the air around me felt like it held a slight electric charge. Cripes. It had to be the new fabric softener I was using.

"That's Min," a man next to me said. "The Egyptian god of fertility."

I smirked. "More like the god of Viagra."

His soft, low chuckle drew my attention. The man was tall, lean like a runner, his dark hair was slicked back, and his gray eyes held a hint of amusement. "He'd be a hard pill to swallow."

My skin buzzed as he gave me an appraising once over. The heat of a blush rose in my cheeks. I forced a bland expression and leveled my gaze at him. "Old Lady Boothwell probably had no gag reflex."

The man grinned, the slight lift in his brow the only sign that I'd surprised him. He leaned in and said with a quiet voice, "She has an assortment of fetish items that border on torture devices, so it wouldn't surprise me."

I pursed my lips. My eyes widening in shock. "She did not."

He laughed and shook his head. "No, she didn't. But wouldn't it have been grand if she had?"

Marigold showed up and slipped her arm in mine. "Hey, I see you've met Keir already." She glanced at the man. "I told you he was gorgeous."

Keir's eyes darted to the right as if looking for an escape route, but he didn't actually try to leave. Instead, he met my gaze. "You must be Iris," he said. "Your sister has told me all about you."

I gave Marigold a soft elbow to the ribs and stifled a groan. "Well, that's ten minutes of your life you'll never be able to get back."

His mouth quirked up on one side. "I know a good time travel spell."

"Isn't that handy," I said, wishing it were true. I would go back in time to the point where I conceived Michael, then I would have dumped Ethan's cheating ass. I shook my head. He hadn't been cheating on me then.

Keir shifted his gaze to a suit-clad man across the room who was waving madly at him. He tilted his head to me, and I couldn't stop myself from admiring the sensuous curve of his lower lip. "I'll be talking to you soon," he said.

"Yes, you will," I answered breathlessly. That's when Marigold's elbow found my ribs. I blinked. "I mean, yes, of course. To talk about the book."

He grinned then and winked. "Is that what the kids are calling it these days?"

Before I could stammer out a response, Keir Quinn strolled off in the direction of the urgently waving man.

"He's really full of himself," I muttered.

My sister laughed. "The lady doth protest too much, methinks."

I reached into my purse and jingled my keys. "I'm going to leave you here to fend for yourself."

She pressed her fingertips into her chest, her eyes wide in mock disbelief. "You wouldn't dare."

"No, I wouldn't," I agreed. "Now distract me with cool stuff before I change my mind."

# CHAPTER 3

"OHHH," MARIGOLD COOED OVER A TALL VIRIDESCENT vase with a fluted opening. The piece, mounted inside a silver holder, was described as a Victorian epergne with a silver-plated stand. "You know how I love green. This would go perfectly on the shelf next to my chaise."

"If you don't mind a little radiation in your reading nook," I told her. The bottom of the tag said it was made of Vaseline glass, a glass with trace amounts of uranium added. We'd made our way from the foyer into the grand dining hall. The room was bigger than my kitchen and dining room combined.

Marigold waved a dismissive hand at me. "It's not like I would drink out of it."

Someone tapped my shoulder. I turned around, but no one was close to me. There were several boxed lots on three buffet tables in the center of the room behind me. Boxed lots usually had a bunch of small things inside that would all be auctioned off as one item. Bidding on them was a lot like panning for gold. Sometimes it was all worthless rocks, but occasionally, there would be a few nuggets to make it worth your while. A crowd of men and women milled around the lots, but no one even glanced in my direction.

I focused my attention back on my sister and her radioactive find.

Another tap.

I turned again.

Again, there was no one.

"What's wrong?" Marigold asked.

"Someone's messing with me." I glared at anyone and everyone in the vicinity. But no one lingered. A woman made eye contact with me then quickly moved on to another room. I noted the hot professor standing under the archway leading into a huge formal dining room. He was engrossed in a serious conversation with the guy in the suit.

"Messing with you how?" Marigold asked.

"Whoever it is, keeps tapping me on the shoulder then ducking away before I turn around."

Marigold scanned the room with me then shrugged. "Maybe it's opportunity knocking," she said. She quirked a brow toward Keir. "Maybe it's the universe trying to get your attention."

"Or maybe it's just some jackass who thinks he or she is a comedian." Even if it was the universe, the way it had been treating me lately, I had zero interest in listening to anything it had to say. I changed the subject. "So, are you going to bid on the vase?"

Marigold touched the base of it and smiled. "I think I will. It really speaks to me."

"I hear wearing a tinfoil hat can put a stop to the voices."

I chuckled when she rolled her eyes. My prankster tapped my shoulder once more.

I whirled around, ready to sock someone in the nose, but still, no one was behind me. "Son of a bitch. Who is this guy? Houdini?"

Marigold's brows dipped. "Iris...I didn't see anyone behind you. Are you sure someone was touching you?"

The expression of concern on my sister's face soured my stomach. "I know what a tap feels like." *Tap tap tap*. Instead of turning this time, I reached back to grab the hand, but my fingers only found my shoulder.

Marigold gave a slight shake of her head as I met her gaze. "I'm telling you, there wasn't anyone there."

I blinked at her, rubbing my arms to stave off a sudden chill. "I swear it felt real."

"You're probably just overly tired." She didn't bring up the divorce, but the implication was there.

"I haven't been getting much sleep," I admitted. Even so, those taps had felt solid and real. I glanced over at the boxes on the tables in the center of the room. There were fewer people around them now.

"I'm going to go check out the boxes," I told my sister.

She gave me a quick nod. "Go ahead. I want to look at the depression glass over here." She pointed to shelves of decorative plates, bowls, and candy dishes on the far wall. She looked at her watch. "If you want, we can split up and meet in the ballroom when the auction starts."

"It's a plan." A feeling of disquiet grew inside me as I looked in the first box on the table nearest me. It had some cookbooks, metal serving spoons, and some kitchen gadgets. I went to the next box on the left, and this noise started in my head like an unpleasant hum. Marigold nailed it when she said I was overly tired. It was the only explanation for all the weirdness I'd been feeling. I rubbed my eyes and gave my head a slight shake. The noise grew louder. I went back to the previous box, and the humming lessened.

I moved back to the second box, and the noise increased. Weird. I went back to the first box. Volume down. Then back to the new box. Volume up.

I made a mental note to call a shrink for an appointment to get my sanity checked. My sister Dahlia would've said I was having psychosomatic symptoms due to emotional trauma, and she'd probably be right. The divorce had sucked, but I'd been ready for it to be over. Maybe signing the paperwork had stressed me out more than I thought it had. The box that hummed was full of bird figurines. Perhaps some of them were Hummels. I'd seen one on the Antiques Roadshow that had been appraised at six hundred dollars.

An unpleasant burning sensation started in my fingertips as I reached into the box, and it traveled through my palm and up my arm. I snatched my hand back. Psychosomatic or not, there was something in me that wanted nothing to do with the porcelain fowl. I moved to the next box on the table. I could still hear a humming sound, but it was more pleasant than the previous one—soothing and, weirdly, inviting.

The box top was folded over. When I drew back the cardboard flap, the first thing that caught my attention was the scent of musty parchment. I smiled as I took in the beautiful sight before me. Old books. There was a hodgepodge-mishmash of leather-bound tomes stacked inside. There were five books, each of them probably eleven by sixteen inches, or thereabouts, in size. There was only enough room in the box to fit four of them stacked together across the bottom with their spines facing out. The fifth book had been set on top with the front cover exposed. I leaned over and inhaled.

"I do love the scent of antique books," a brunette woman next to me said. "There is a romance to holding and reading from pages that have been inked by hand or an old-fashioned iron press."

She looked at me as if she knew me, but I didn't recognize her. "Do we know each other?"

She studied me for a moment, then smiled. "I think we do. You're Mrs. Callahan, right? You were my instructor for freshman composition at Darling U."

"Oh my gosh, that would have been at least seventeen years ago."

"Eighteen," she said with a laugh. "But who's counting." She held out her hand. "Luanne Danvers, but call me, Lu. All my friends do."

I shook her hand. "Please call me, Iris. I haven't been a teacher in so long." And I was no longer Mrs. Callahan, but I wasn't going into that. "Do you live in Southill now?"

"I recently got a divorce," she said solemnly. "I needed a change, and I had some fond memories of this town from my college days, so I moved here."

"Just like that, huh?" I could see the appeal of running away from an old life. "No kids then?"

"Nope, just me." She smiled. "Hey, if you ever get bored, I'd love to hang out."

"Sure," I said as she was pulling out her phone. She

handed it to me. "Just put your number in there. I'll text you later, so you have mine."

"Sounds good." I put my name and number in her contacts and handed the phone back to her.

"These books are great," she said. "You planning on bidding on them?"

"Maybe." I brushed my fingertips across the cover of the top book. "I wonder how old this one is?" The embossed leather was soft to the touch without any of the cracking that can happen with age. Mrs. Boothwell had taken exceptionally good care of the book. Sewn-in silver thread added a quilted quality to the borders, and there wasn't a single popped stitch. My heart raced with anticipation. "Wow. This cover is mint."

"They're not worth much," Keir Quinn said louder than necessary, joining Lu and me at the table. "But I can see the sentimental value in them for a collector."

I gave him a sharp look. "These are old and in great shape. They have more than sentimental value."

He shrugged. "I wouldn't give more than twenty, maybe thirty dollars for them."

After his proclamation, several people who'd been waiting for me to leave the box moved on to other items. His low estimation of the value had focused their attention elsewhere.

I arched a brow at him, and he smiled. "You're welcome." He pulled a card from his front pocket with his name and a phone number printed on the front. "I hope you'll return the favor by texting me to set up a meeting to talk about my book. From what your sister says, you're the best non-fiction editor around, and I could desperately use your service."

"I'm the only non-fiction editor around here." I studied Keir for a moment. He had chiseled good looks that I was certain most people found charming and hard to resist. I was not most people. "I bet there's not a desperate bone in your body."

"Not a single desperate bone, huh?" He chuckled, and the sound was like Marvin Gaye's music on steroids. In other words, it was sexy as hell.

"I didn't mean—" I shook my head. My cheeks flushed with heat as I shifted focus to the leather-bound tome. A symbol of an upside-down triangle with a horizontal line across the bottom half just above the point decorated the cover. Was that always there? I didn't recall seeing it when I first looked at the book, but I'd been understandably a little scatterbrained today. "Do you know what this is?"

"I do," he replied.

I waited for him to elaborate.

He didn't.

"Well?" I asked. "What is it?"

Keir tipped his head to me. "Call me," he said. "I'll be happy to trade my knowledge for some of yours." On that note, he gave a slight bow and walked to the next room.

Lu grinned at me. "I think you have an admirer."

"I hardly know the guy," I denied.

"Sometimes chemistry is instant," Lu said. "There's a few things I want to check out upstairs before this event gets going. Let's get together soon."

"You got it," I told her.

"Hot, right?" my sister said in my ear when she came up behind me.

"Luanne?"

"Who's Luanne?"

"The woman I was just talking to, dope."

Marigold shook her head. "I was talking about Keir, dope," she countered. "I told you you'd like him."

I set the book back in the box and noted the lot number on my bidding sheet. "And you were wrong then and wrong now. I don't like him at all."

"But you agree he's sexy as hell."

I pursed my lips for a moment, then acquiesced. "He's definitely sexy." Before she could get too excited, I added, "But too slick for my taste."

Marigold wiggled her brows. "I'm sure he tastes like blue diamonds and green clovers."

"Don't ruin Lucky Charms for me."

"The auction will start in ten minutes," a man announced. "Bidding will take place in the ballroom. Please follow the red arrows."

"Did you find anything you want?" I asked Marigold.

"I have my eye on the Vaseline vase, an incense diffuser that looks like it had been crafted for the Dalai Lama himself, and a beaded chandelier that would look awesome in my meditation room." Marigold nodded to me. "You?"

"Oh, I have my eye on something." I folded the top of the box closed. "And if I'm really lucky, I won't have to spend more than twenty bucks to get it."

# CHAPTER 4

It was after nine and dark by the time we got home, and I had enlisted my strapping teenager to haul my auction bootie into the house. "Christ, Mom," Michael complained. "Did you buy a box of bricks?"

"Close," I told him. "You got the first and last letters right."

He groaned. "How many freaking books do you need?"

"Quit giving your mom a hard time," Marigold said. "Sure, we might see her on one of those reality tv shows someday where the hosts are hauling crap out of her house..."

She let the implication linger. I shook my head. I had full bookshelves in my living room and in my bedroom, but as long as there was room to walk around, there was room for more books. "I like to push the boundaries between collecting and hoarding."

Michael plunked the lot box down on the coffee table. "Mission accomplished."

I walked over to him and tugged on his arm. He dipped his face so I could kiss his cheek. "Thank you for the muscle, babe."

He grunted and gave a light shrug.

Marigold, who had finished moving her auction finds to her car, walked into the house behind us. She nudged Michael with her shoulder. "You excited about your senior year?"

"I don't know," he muttered on another shrug. My son was at an age where most questions from anyone older than eighteen were viewed as a challenge. I could ask him how his day was, and he'd act like I'd accused him of murder. I stuck to statements when talking to the kid.

Marigold accepted the answer and moved on to her next question. "You got any summer plans?"

Michael flashed a quick look at me then shook his head. "Not really."

"Are you seeing anyone?"

His eyes widened like a deer in the headlights. A large part of me wanted to rescue my boy from his aunt's interrogation. However, a smaller part of me wanted to see the kid squirm a little, but I suppressed that part.

I flicked my fingers in Marigold's direction. "Tell your aunt good night."

The corner of his mouth quirked up. "Night, Aunt Marigee."

"Goodnight, baby boy." She winked at him. After Michael left the room, she turned her attention back to me. "He's not really going to bed, right? When I was his age, I never saw the backside of my eyelids until well after midnight. Even on school nights."

"He has practice early tomorrow morning, but I'm sure he'll be playing video games into the wee hours. I was just throwing him a lifeline." I stroked the top of the lot box, my fingers itching to get to the contents. "However, I'm going to call it an early night." I yawned dramatically. "Big day today. I'm exhausted."

Marigold shook her head. She gave me a bland look. "You're right. It was a big day. You had to put on a whole bra and leave the house."

I chucked a throw pillow from the couch at her.

Marigold laughed as she easily caught the fluffy projectile. She held it arms-length to look at the front. "Oh my gosh." Her eyes widened. "These are not cabbage flowers."

I snickered. "Nope."

"And what does your son think about having decorative penises on the couch."

"I've had it on the couch since December. He hasn't even noticed. Not once." I glanced around the room. "An editor friend of mine from Kentucky sent it to me at Christmas time for a laugh."

"Did it work?"

I smiled. "It did."

"So..." My sister tapped her chin as she strolled toward my auction haul. "What's so special about the books that prompted you to get in a bidding war with a seventy-year-old used bookstore owner?"

"I wanted to punch Mr. Jarlsberg in his bifocals," I muttered. The old guy had been determined to win, but not at any cost. Two hundred dollars had been his limit, so I'd won the bid for the not-so-low price of two-hundred and one dollars. "I'm just glad no one else wanted them."

Marigold tossed the penis pillow onto the couch and flipped the top cardboard flap open.

I swatted it down. "Hey, don't touch my box."

She raised her hands in surrender then eyed me suspiciously. "Did you find a first edition of Shakespeare's Folio in there?"

"I wish." I snorted. One had sold the previous year for almost ten million dollars. "I'd be set for life." I sat down on the couch. "Honestly, I don't know what I'm going to find in there. I only looked at the top book, and I have no idea what it's about." I frowned at Marigold. "Have you ever had a moment when you saw something, and you just knew you had to have it?"

"The last time that happened to me, I ended up spending a Saturday afternoon in a free clinic."

I snorted a laugh. "I don't think anything in this box will require a penicillin shot."

My sister arched her brow and smirked. "You say that now."

I stood back up and started walking to the door. "If I end up with a rash, I'll call you."

"All right. I get it." Marigold backed up toward the exit. "You want to be alone with your dusty old books."

The minute she was out the door, and it was closed between us, I stripped off my bra and sat back down on the couch. I rubbed my hands together like a maniacal supervillain. It had more to do with the way my skin tingled around the box more than any vision of world domination. I glanced around the room to make sure I was alone as if I were doing something wrong. Taking a deep breath, I centered myself.

Why couldn't I shake off the feeling of excitement, anticipation, and even a little danger?

The leather-bound book with the upside-down triangle with the line sat undisturbed on the top of the other books. I carefully lifted it from the container just in case it was more fragile than it appeared. The other four books in the box were literary omnibuses. Nothing too exciting, but I was glad to add them to my collection. However, those could wait until later.

As I placed the mysterious tome on my lap, a mighty whoosh as if I'd just driven my car eighty miles an hour over the top of a steep hill rushed through my body. The burst of adrenaline made my hands cold and shaky as I opened the book to the first page. A handwritten inscription was centered at the top.

*Blood of my blood, a sacrifice required.*

*Tears of my tears bring what's most desired.*

*A journey not entered lightly. Magick you must hold tightly.*

*Once it's begun, it cannot be undone.*

*Goddess, help you.*

I blinked at the final line and blew out a breath I'd been holding. "That's not ominous or anything."

A sting on my left index finger made me jerk my hand out from under the book. A smear of blood coated my fingertip. I flipped the cover shut to see what I'd cut myself on.

A barb of silver thread poked out from the stitching on the top border. I wouldn't have noticed it if it weren't for the dark spot where my blood had colored the leather.

"Shoot." I rushed the book to the kitchen and placed it on the table before rifling through my towel drawer for a white washcloth. Other than a quick rinse of my finger to make sure the wound wasn't more than a tiny prick, I kept my focus on the book. I needed to get the bloodstain out before it set and ruined the mint condition of the leather. I ran cold water over the terrycloth and wrung out the excess. Quickly, I dabbed the damp cloth onto the affected spot and nearly jabbed myself a second time.

"Son of a bitch."

"What are you doing?" Michael asked.

I jumped because until he'd spoken, I hadn't even noticed he'd come into the kitchen. I turned around to face him and slid the book so that it was partially hidden. "Cripes, son. I'm going to put a bell around your neck."

"You're so weird," he said as he grabbed a bottle of juice from the fridge. He threw the cap into the trash then left without a second glance in my direction.

I'd tried to hide the book from him. But why? I'd done it instinctually and without any thought. I'd also slapped the top flap down on the box earlier when my sister had tried to get a peek at the book. I faced the leather-bound tome, the excitement from earlier returning.

*Oh my, gawd, I'm turning into Golem, and this book is my precioussss.*

So be it. I scooped the precious up and carried it out the back door to the garden. It was dark out, but the garden was lit with fairy lights. Plenty bright enough for me to do a cursory examination. However, I grabbed a small flashlight and a magnifying glass from the kitchen drawer in case I needed them.

I sat down on the bench, and the stupid gnome, was

staring at me. I was going to ground Michael until he graduated from college.

"Stop staring at me, Linda," I told the stony thorn in my ass. "It's mine." I stroked the cover again. "All mine." I glared at the gnome, its beady eyes twinkling in the glow of the fairy lights. "Don't judge me." I hoped the new feeling of obsession was divorce-related and not my sanity leaving the building.

I opened the book once more and tried to shake off the feeling of crazy.

The page after the inscription was blank. I flipped to the next, then the next, and so on until I was absolutely certain. They were all blank.

"What in the world?" I'd been so excited after that initial inscription. Every fiber of my being had been jazzed as if I were on the verge of something amazing. I clapped the book shut. "That sucks."

"You're a dunce," someone said. The voice was low and graveled.

I darted my gaze around the dimly lit garden. "Michael?" It hadn't sounded like him, but he'd taken great joy in startling me at the most unexpected times. "I swear, if you don't show yourself, I'm going to take your video games away." It was the most expedient threat to get a response from him. But no gotcha followed.

"Hey, floppy-tits! If you want to invoke your grimoire, you have to make your intention known," the disembodied voice growled.

"Nope." I jumped to my feet. "I have a gun." My threat was empty. I didn't actually have a gun, and even if I did, I wouldn't carry it on me.

"I'm quaking in my winklepickers."

I held the book tightly to my chest. None of the plants were tall enough to hide a grown human, and my backyard garden was small. Unless the voice belonged to a ghost, I was having an auditory hallucination. One that called me floppy tits and said things like winklepickers. "There's no one here," I told myself. "I'm suffering a psychotic break induced by divorce. Plain and simple."

"You're right about one thing." A rock hit my shins. I looked down and saw my bearded, pink-clad gnome, Linda, in the flesh and flipping me the bird. "You really are plain and simple."

# CHAPTER 5

"SIT DOWN, DROOPY-BOOBS, BEFORE YOU PASS OUT." THE gnome had a slight accent, German in origin if I were to hazard a guess.

I sat back down on the bench, and not because I was obeying an inanimate object that had suddenly animated. It had more to do with the fact that the ground felt as if it were shifting under my feet.

"There you go," the gnome said. "Deep breaths now."

Every word it said made me even dizzier. "Stop talking."

"Too late for that, lazy apples."

I pressed my palms into my forehead. "What is your obsession with my breasts?"

"You're the one who insists on going au natural." The tiny, bearded asshole waved its hands around its chest to emphasize.

"I'm having a nightmare." I squeezed my eyes shut. "This isn't real. This is the result of day-old takeout, the divorce, and a lack of sleep. Any minute, I'm going to wake up."

Sharp pain on my forearm grabbed my attention. "Ow." I glared at the gnome, who was making pincer motions with her index finger and thumb.

"Not a dream, baggy—"

I snapped my fingers. "Enough of that." I wore a B cup for Pete's sake. If there was any sagging at all, it was minimal. "If you're going to insist on talking to me, the least you can do is keep your not-so-flattering nicknames to yourself."

"You're going to have to develop a thicker skin if you want to learn the secrets of terra-craft."

"Michael!" I yelled.

"Why are you calling the boy?"

"I'm going to need him to call nine-one-one."

"Go to Southill Village, they said," the gnome lamented. "It will be fun, they said."

I narrowed my gaze on the wee monster. "Who's they?"

"My donsy, of course. We felt your power at your birth, and I followed you here to this goddess-forsaken mountain crap-hole."

There was a lot to process in what the gnome just said, but first I had to know... "What's a donsy?"

"A group of gnomes, ignorant *Kleinkind*."

I was reasonably sure *Kleinkind* wasn't a compliment, but at least, it wasn't another derogatory nickname for my boobs. "And what are winklepickers?"

"Technically, their *crakows*." It picked up one of its feet and gestured to its pointy shoe. "But the more modern version of the long, pointy-toed shoe is called a winklepicker. I picked these suckers up in London, England, back in the sixties."

I groaned. "So, what's your name?"

"Linda is fine." The gnome tugged its beard. "I've gotten used to it these past few years. Besides, my real name is impossible to pronounce."

I got the feeling Linda wasn't telling me something important. "Are you a...boy gnome?"

"Even if I were male, I wouldn't be a boy. I'm old enough to have seen two centuries come and go, *Kleinkind*."

"You didn't tell me what a *Kleinkind* was."

"I'm not here to teach you German. You can look it up on your own time."

Aha! I was right about the German. "So, you're a girl... er...female, I mean."

"I'm a gnomide, yes," Linda agreed. "A female of my kind." She shook her head. "I was certain the beard gave it away."

"Don't all gnomes have beards?"

She gave me a withering glare. "Of course." She followed up with a string of foreign expletives that made me cringe. "I'm not here to school you in gnome gendering, either."

Some of the shock had worn off, and annoyance was setting in. "Then what the hell are you here for? I mean, if it's to point the way to a pot of gold at the end of a rainbow, lead the way. Otherwise, what good are you?"

Linda's cheeks turn the color of beets. "I am not a leprechaun, you giant pimple on my ass. I'm a gnome. A powerful earth spirit. I have fought in two major wars against *die Hexenmeister*, and I have tutored over twenty warrior witches in terra-craft." She shook her tiny fist at me. "Call me a leprechaun one more time."

I didn't know whether to be afraid of Linda or not. On the one hand, she was a foot tall and weighed twenty pounds when she was stone. How much damage could she do? On the other hand, she was walking and talking, and who knew what other tricks she might have up her sleeves. I decided, as my therapist would call it, to de-escalate. "Chill your panties, Linda. I didn't mean anything by it. I just figured you were all in the same family of...whatever you are."

"We are not. Leprechauns are fairies and not even one of the good kinds." Her tone suggested she was still grudging. "But I'll let it go for now."

"Did you say you were going?"

"This is where I live, stupid witch," Linda said. "I felt your potential all the way across the ocean when you were born, but I'm worried it will never develop. You are too closed off to the veil. You can't master tru-craft with a limited mind."

"My mind is not limited," I said defensively. My brows pinched together. "Did you say witch?"

She ignored me. "The best I can hope for is to teach you enough to keep you from becoming aether dust."

"I don't know what that means."

"It means..." Linda scooped up a handful of dirt from the rosemary bed and sprinkled it on the paving stones. "...the magic will burn through you like you are puking and crapping solar flares until your flesh and bones turn to a magical ash that will recycle your magic into the world." The gnome scratched her head. "Come to think of it, that might not be a bad alternative."

I didn't try to hide my horror. "Speak for yourself."

"What do you think I'm doing?" She gave me a complete, duh, look. "I would never speak for anyone else."

"I am going to wake up soon, and this horrible nightmare is going to be over."

"If you don't wake up soon and jump-start your magic, you're going to get more of a nightmare than you ever imagined. There are forces in the world that want what you have. If you don't fight for it, they will take it from you."

"Before or after I turn to dust?"

"Yes," Linda replied.

"Magic isn't real."

"Neither are talking gnomes," she said, beating me to the punch. "But here we are. You're going to have to readjust your way of thinking about reality, *Kleinkind*. And fast. If you don't, you won't survive the transformation."

"I don't want to transform."

"You should've thought about that before you blooded the grimoire."

"I did what?"

"You melded your blood with the magic. The book is glowing with the spark of power. It just needs your intention."

I shook my head. "Why now? If it's true that I was born with magic, why am I just seeing it now." In fiction books, these kinds of things always happened to someone on the precipice of adulthood. Usually, someone more my son's age than mine. "I'm forty-three years old, after all. Not some young babe reaching a milestone age."

The gnome drew closer to me, and she placed her bitty palm on my arm. She closed her eyes, the lines around them creasing deeply as she hummed. When she finished, she took a step away. "You weren't ready before."

"And I am now?" I snorted. "Hah. That's awfully convenient. I mean, if old Mrs. Boothwell hadn't died, I'd have never bought the books, and all this weird crap wouldn't be happening right now." A thought jumped into my head. "The book." I slid it off my lap and onto the bench beside me. "That batty old woman laced it with some kind of drug. A hallucinogen like PCP or LSD. My lord! That accounts for all of this. Even the feelings I was getting during and after the auction. "I'm drugged!" I said the last as if I were declaring, Eureka!

"Right now, I could use some drugs," Linda said sardonically. "It might be the only thing that keeps me from strangling you."

I giggled. "I don't think you can get your micro-fingers around my neck."

A loud meow startled me. A small, fluffy animal skittered across my yard. I eeped, but just as quickly, the damn thing ran into my house. It had been a cat, right? I mean, I'd heard a meow, but it had been hard to tell. Why was my back door open? I was sure I'd shut it when I went outside. Of course, I'd been eager to study the book, and I was on drugs, so maybe I hadn't. Cripes, this acid trip was doing my head in. "Did you just see a cat run in my house?" I felt woozy.

Linda threw up her hands and stomped around. "You're no good to me like this. And you're definitely no good to yourself. You might as well go to bed. We'll get at it early tomorrow morning after Michael leaves for practice."

The fact that the gnome knew my son's schedule was another vote for drugs. "That's a grand idea, Linda." I left the book on the bench so that I wouldn't contaminate myself with whatever substance had been smeared on it and walked into my house. "I'm going to bed."

"I'll be seeing you in the morning, *Kleinkind.*"

I winked at her as I staggered inside. "Not if I see you first."

# CHAPTER 6

I HAD PASSED BY SEVERAL TREES BEFORE I REALIZED I WAS walking in a forest. No cedar or pine, for sure. So not anywhere on the mountain where I lived. I'd gone to bed, right? Yeah. I am pretty sure I'd fallen face-first onto my pillow without even taking off my clothes. *Whew*. Whatever drugs the old lady had used on those books was really kicking in hard. If there was an afterlife, I'm sure she was out there somewhere laughing her wrinkled ass off at me.

I wish I could say this was the first time I'd experienced being on a hallucinogenic. Once in college, I'd accidentally taken shrooms. In my defense, I thought they were dried shitakes. Seeing things that weren't there scared the crap out of me. Turns out, I wasn't a roll with the psychedelic flow kind of gal. Luckily, my roommate, Ashley Porter, had stayed with me the whole night, reminding me to breathe and remain calm.

"Take deep breaths," she'd said. "None of this is real. It can't hurt you."

For whatever reason, Ashley had looked like an angel in my delusions with full halo and wings. It'd been easy to trust an angel. But now, it seemed, I was alone on this drug-induced journey. It was harder to believe it wasn't real, and it wouldn't hurt me.

Wet moss squished between my toes as I focused on staying relaxed and riding this high out to its conclusion. That is until I heard a woman's voice through the trees.

"Earth beneath me, sustaining life. Air around me, breathing life. Fire above me, authority of life. Water within me, refreshing life." By the end of the incantation, a vocalized song of joy swelled. I didn't know how many voices had enjoined to create the wordless music, but the harmonies were pitch perfect.

This hallucination was getting trippier by the minute. A full moon appeared in the sky and lit a path through the trees. My brain said nothing good ever happens when you go into the light, but my body was like, *weeeee*, a light!

"Your body is on drugs, too," I reminded myself. But as the chorus of lovely sounds grew louder and more insistent, my movement toward down the lit path became less of a want and more of a need.

One moment I was surrounded by dense trees, and the next, I was stepping out into an open field with five tall obelisks arranged in a circle. Inside the ring, there were eleven people in robes and a twelfth standing at an altar of sorts. It was tall enough to reach the woman's hips and it looked like it was made of four stacked slab stones that were white in color and glowed like a beacon.

Again, my brain told me to stay put, but my heart told

my brain to go to hell as I traversed the field toward the beautiful song and radiant circle.

The singing stopped.

"Come, child," a robed woman near the altar said. She had blonde hair, and there were symbols carved into her face on her cheeks, chin, and forehead.

"That had to hurt," I said.

She looked confused for a moment, then smiled as she touched her cheeks. "Welcome, Iris Everlee of Southill Village, descendant of Islandmagee. We have been waiting for you." Her voice was like silk against my skin, and I was betting if she pulled back her hood and took off her robe, she, like my roommate, would have a halo and wings.

"Are you an angel, too?"

"Do you meet many angels?" she asked.

"Only when I'm tripping balls," I replied.

She gave me a tight smile. "This druid circle has been convened to welcome you, child of Earth and aide you in your transformation."

Druids had not been on my Drug Delusions' bingo list. "Uhm, thanks, I guess."

The woodsy scent of heather and lavender, a combination of masculine and feminine, surrounded me as I was suddenly inside the circle. I glanced around at the other robed figures, but the shadows cast by their cowls made it hard to see any faces. I should've been scared—an intelligent person would have been. But I wasn't. Because, you know, *acid* trip.

Runic carvings decorated the surface of the white altar. On the flat top was a circle of small dark stones, a bowl of water, incense, and candles.

"Are you ready?" the woman asked me.

I shrugged. "Sure."

"Name your intention."

Not that nonsense. Linda had told me that I needed to make my intention known. I had no idea what she'd been talking about. I still didn't. But this was my hallucination. Maybe that meant there was something inside my subconscious or in my psyche that did. Perhaps it had been in one of the textbooks I'd edited. Intention sounded very much like a psychology thing. But the last psych book I'd covered was two years ago, and its focus had been on child psychology. I'd found it interesting because I could see things in Michael that the book talked about as far as ages and stages went. Still, I didn't remember any specific part that talked about intention.

"I don't understand what you want." Or maybe it was what I wanted. No. What I wanted was for this drug to metabolize its way out of my system so I could get on with my life. I made a mental note to go to the emergency room when I found my way back to reality, so I could get my blood tested. I would need the evidence for when I sued the Boothwell estate and the auction house for poisoning me. Luckily, I knew a lawyer who would take the case on the cheap. "What do you want me to say?"

"The words matter not, my child. The magic will know your heart."

I almost laughed. It had been over a year since I'd had anything more than pain and resentment in my heart. I wasn't sure that was an intention I wanted to put out there. "I think I'd prefer magic to mind its own business?"

There was a chuckle from someone in the robed circle.

The woman, who I assumed was the boss since she was doing all the talking, gave the offender an admonishing glance before turning her attention back to me.

"My dear, it doesn't work that way." The woman waved her hands in the air. Shimmering trails of sparkly dust floated above her. "Now that your magic has been activated, it must have an intention or it becomes wild."

"Is that such a bad thing?"

"Wild magic grows like weeds, choking the life out of everything in its path."

I remembered what Linda had said about magic burning through me, and I'd puke and fart solar flares. Oh my, gawd. Was the sparkly haze above this woman someone who'd burned so hot they turned to ash? I focused on keeping my breath slow, and even as I reminded myself, this was a hallucination. But, holy crap, the mounting panic attack felt pretty freaking real.

"I don't feel very well."

"Choose, Iris," the woman said with more insistence.

"Between what?"

"The grimoire has chosen your tru-craft. Your element is terra." She gestured to crystals on the altar. "Pick one. It will know your intention."

I was beginning to hate that word. "What are my options? I mean, other than wild choking weeds."

"There are two disciplines of mage, the Fade and the Bright. Your intent—"

I held up a hand to stop her. "Fade and Bright. What's the difference? Is that like black and white magic? Bad and good?"

"There is no such thing as bad or good magic. But the

Fade and the Bright are opposite sides of the same coin. One cannot exist without the other. Your true heart will choose for you if you cannot. Please," she gestured to the crystals more insistently. "Take one."

I noticed she wasn't touching the crystals. Maybe they were laced with drugs as well. Could I get drugged by a delusion? Probably not. But why take a chance? "I'm the kind of woman who has to read over a contract four or five times and run it past my lawyer before I commit to anything. I'll pass."

"I insist," the bossy blonde said.

Next thing I knew, I was inches from the altar. So, trippy. "You first," I said.

She gave me a bland look then snapped her fingers. One of the robed underlings strolled to the altar and picked up one of the crystals. The hands were large, masculine, but well-manicured. As he reached out to take the offering, I noted a dark mark, possibly a scar, in a shape similar to a star on his wrist. He grasped the clear crystal, holding his hand in a tight fist around the gemstone. A surge of energy zipped through me then it was gone. When he turned his hand supine and opened his fingers, the clear crystal had turned a luminescent white.

"Is that the Bright?"

She nodded and gestured for another of her robed minions to come over. This one had more delicate hands with slender fingers. This one had a nice manicure, too, but it was harder to tell if the person was a woman or a man. The process was repeated. The minion grasped the crystal, energy spiked, and when the crystal was revealed, it looked like a crystal-cut piece of onyx.

"Neat." My eyes widened. "I take it that's the Fade?"

"Very good," the woman said. "Now it's your turn."

I took a step back. "I thought you said it wasn't about black or white magic? I've never been a religious person but really don't want to be putting any evil crap out into the world." Once more, I was only inches from the altar. Well, damn it.

"Do you want to die, child?" she asked.

"I do not," I admitted. Although, there was a good chance I was half-dead and lying in my backyard right now. I remembered walking into the house, but then I was here in this super flat forest that wasn't anywhere near a mountain. So...chances were good, I'd overdosed on whatever I'd been exposed to. I chose to be optimistic about my survival, though. After all, I was still self-aware. That was a good thing, right? "What if I change my mind later? Can I change from Bright to Fade? You know, like my very own mood rocks. Black for when I'm ready to kill my ex, and white for when I'm watching my kid tackle a quarterback?"

"Oh, for Bec's sake." The blonde's exasperation made her glow, and not in a soothing way. "It's for your own safety and the safety of those around you. When I say your magic will suffocate the life around you if you let it go wild, I mean your life and the life of those you love. Think of your son, Iris, and pick up the damn crystal."

I held up my hands in surrender. "Sheesh, okay. Don't go nuclear or anything." I tapped the nearest crystal, one about the size of my thumb, the way someone might tap a stovetop to make sure it wasn't hot.

It wasn't hot. Or cold, for that matter. There were no

sparks or pain or any explosions as I plucked it from the surface and placed it in the palm of my hand. "Now what?"

"Close your eyes and will your int..." She shook her head. "Just close your eyes and think of what makes you who you are. What are your best characteristics? What are the things in life that are most important to you? That will make your role in our world clear."

"Or cloudy. Get it," I jested. "Because the crystal turns opaque."

The woman didn't look amused.

"All right," I told her. "If squeezing this piece of quartz will get me out of this crazy fantasy, I'll give it a go."

I curled my fingers slowly around the piece. There was no energy like with the other two people. Was I doing something wrong?

"You have to think," the blonde said.

"Got it. Think."

What made me who I am? I'd been found when I was a few weeks old. My mother had said I'd been surrendered, aka abandoned to a hospital in Briarberry Falls, a town on the other side of the mountain. No family came forward to claim me, so I'd gone into the system. My mother, Grace Everlee, had been friends with the child protection officer and had taken me in as a foster. She and my dad, Randall Everlee, officially adopted me fourteen months later. I'd been a blank slate. Someone without a name. Without any legacy. My parents had changed that for me. In a way, it was their generosity that had made me the person I'd grown into.

But there was also Evan. I'd met him in college, and with him, I became something more than what my parents had made me. I became a lover, a wife, and a mother. And his cheating had shaped me even more. Was there a core part of me that stayed static? My head hurt considering all the possibilities. So instead, I focused on characteristics.

I was detail-oriented. It made me really good at my job as an editor. I had empathy, which sometimes didn't feel like a good thing. It meant I cared about other people, but sometimes those feelings overwhelmed me. My father said I was a fighter from the get-go and that he could tell from the moment he first laid eyes on me that I would be his little warrior. I think it was his nice way of saying I was stubborn as hell. My mom always told me I was smart and that with my brains, I could accomplish anything I set my mind to.

I thought about my current predicament. Divorced, living like a hermit, and having a hallucination that would've sent Janis Joplin running for rehab.

A pulsing force rushed from my fist up my arm and into my body. I felt electrified with power as the exhilaration washed over me. The wind kicked up around me, blowing my hair across my face. It startled me enough to falter, and the energy began to ebb.

"No, keep going, Iris," the woman said. "It is here. Let your fear go, and your life can begin anew."

I shook my head. I liked my life. I didn't want to start over. Only, signing those divorce papers had pretty much solidified that I was getting a do-over, whether I liked it or not.

I held up my hand, and the ground beneath my feet trembled. "Earth," I whispered.

"That's it, young one," a man said.

I felt a hand on my shoulder, then another on my arm, and another and another. I didn't have to open my eyes to know the robed circle had gathered near my position, and they were all touching me. Oddly, I wasn't scared by their presence. They had the opposite effect. For the first time in months, I felt supported and safe.

I held the crystal tighter as the dirt, the trees, and the rocks all sang. I understood with utter clarity that they contained all the answers to the universe. I had but to listen. A mound of dirt and grass grew over my feet. Vines weaved their way up from the ground and wrapped themselves slowly around my ankles, encircling my legs. I expected the panic to return, but it didn't. Like the hands that were on me, the vines acted as a kind of security blanket. Or at least they felt that way. I didn't even blink twice as the persistent ivy wrapped around my waist and my chest and slithered out onto my arms.

It was only when it began to cover my face that I...

My eyes snapped open. "This is wrong."

I struggled to get loose from the snaking greenery turning me into a bad version of Batman's nemesis, Poison Ivy.

"You are ready, Iris," the woman said. "It's time to let go."

"I can't," I told her.

"Let go, Iris," she insisted. "Let go now."

I struggled to open my hand, but when I finally managed, the stone was...gray. "I don't understand." The look of consternation on the woman's perfect brow told me she was confused as well. "What does this mean?"

"We shall meet again, Iris. And when we do, you must have mastered Earth magic. If you don't—" She spread her arms out as if that were some kind of explanation.

"If I don't...then what?" Before I could get an answer, the

vine around my neck yanked me, and I lost my balance and fell backward.

"Until we next meet," was the last thing I heard before my alarm clock went off at six in the morning.

"Oh, gawd," I murmured. My head felt as if someone had bludgeoned me with a baseball bat. I blinked as I smacked the snooze button. Maybe Michael would get himself up for practice. It could happen, right? Momma had a doozy of a hangover. What in the world had that old lady laced the book with? I would have thrown it in the fireplace if it wasn't for the fact that I might need it as evidence when I sued the pants off of whoever I could sue. But first, I needed to get Michael up and off to practice. I would go to the hospital after. My brother Rowan, named for both the Rowan tree and for his shock of red hair, was a family practitioner in town, and I knew he'd order the test for me without too much fanfare.

The distant sound of a motorboat gave me pause. I lived nowhere near a lake. The sound was persistent and growing louder.

And it was right behind me. I turned as fast as my achy head would let me.

Meow. I vaguely remembered a cat running into the house last night. At least that part hadn't been a hallucination. The white and orange ball of fluff was nesting on what used to be Evan's side of the bed, staring at me with its big green eyes and happily purring as if it had hit the mother lode.

"Get off my bed," I told it. The cat flopped over onto its back, and I could see now that it had two tiny balls between its back legs. "Congratulations," I said. "It's a boy." I scratched his belly. I couldn't help myself. He was super cute, and his dopey expression made him even more adorable. Evan had been allergic to cats and dogs, so we never had any pets.

I rolled onto my back and made a mental note to call a veterinarian today. I would see if the cat was chipped and had an owner, and if it didn't, maybe I'd keep him. Or maybe not. I decided it was best not to make any decisions until I was sure I was no longer under the influence.

I sat up and swung my legs off the bed until I was sitting up. My feet itched, so I pulled the left one up first and set it on my right knee.

"Oh." I blinked as my stomach knotted. My hand shook as I reached down and plucked an ivy leaf from between my dirt-crusted toes. Was I still seeing delusions?

Michael knocked on my bedroom door then poked his head in. "Hey, mom. I'm catching a ride with Doug. We're going to run before practice." His brow dipped when his gaze shifted to my feet. "Did you do some barefoot gardening this morning?"

"So, you see this? You see the dirt on my feet?" I asked him.

"Yeah, I'm not blind." He gave me the "duh" look. He shook his head at me. "I have to go."

"Uhm, sure," I told him absently. "Have a good day."

He closed the door harder than necessary, and the slam made me jump. I looked around for the cat. Michael hadn't mentioned the cat.

"Where are you?"

I felt a whisker against my right ankle as he scooted out from under the bed.

I scratched his head as I contemplated what it meant that I had dirt on my feet and leaves between my toes, but remarkably there were no tracks of soil and foliage on the floor. How had I gotten into bed with muddy feet without leaving a trail?

The cat growled, and I could feel his hackles raise.

"I'll smite you, impudent imp," a familiar voice said. "I don't even need a good reason."

Oh, hell. Linda. "You're not real," I said.

The little asshole, standing in my bedroom doorway, ignored me. "Out of bed, *Kleinkind.* Your child is not the only one who needs to practice."

"I hate you, Linda."

"I don't care if you hate me, as long as you mind me," Linda threw the words I'd used with Michael back at me. The cat hissed at her, and Linda pulled a knife from her pink tunic. "None of that, or I'll be having imp sushi for breakfast."

"Okay, then," I said, throwing back the covers. "Psychotic break, round two."

# CHAPTER 7

I GOT UP, IGNORING THE PROVERBIAL ELEPHANT, OR IN this case, gnome, in the room. Linda wasn't real. She was outside in my garden, and the thing that was following me to the bathroom, and using some pretty colorful language, was part of my delusion.

"Begone," I told her as I poured my first cup of coffee. I had gone to half-caf because of an ulcer I recently developed.

"I would love to, but I can't go until I know you won't do anything catastrophically stupid."

I burned my tongue as I took a sip of coffee. "Like what?" I blew inside the rim then set the cup down.

Linda's lips thinned in a tight grimace. "Like leveling the mountain."

"Okay."

"Did you hear what I said?" the gnome demanded.

"I did," I told her. "Which is why I'm pretty sure leveling

a mountain with magic," I wiggled my fingers around, "is the least of my problems."

If the drug screen came back negative, I would have to see if our family psychologist would give me a discount. The cat jumped up on my counter. It was missing a tail. "Did someone cut it off?" I examined the nub. It flicked back and forth as he quickly turned and rubbed his head against my hand. "You are a sweetie."

"He's a dolt," Linda said. She pointed to her pointy hat. "Nothing between the ears. Much like his witch."

"That's a terrible thing to say," I cooed at the floofy little love bug. "You're such a smart boy."

"He literally isn't," Linda said. "It's by design."

"What's by design?"

"Imps are empty vessels. Tools for witches, and not much good for anything else."

The cat caught sight of a fly, and it leaped off the counter, catching the fly mid-air then landing on the ground, the insect still trapped between its two front paws.

"Hah!" I gestured to the cat. "He caught that sucker in one go." I shook my head. "Not much good for anything else, huh? He's a freaking hunter. A mighty little warrior who will have my house pest-free in no time."

Halfway through my victory speech, the cat rolled onto his back and opened his paws. The fly, apparently unharmed, flew away.

Linda snickered. "Yep, he's a ferocious beast."

The cat flipped to its feet and pounced at something else under the table. "There," I said. "He just had bigger prey to go after."

"Heavens be praised," Linda said as she plucked the cat's spoils from the ground. "He has made your home safe from this rubber band. Never more will the foul creature wreak havoc upon your domain." She placed the rubber band on the tip of her finger and shot it at the trash bin. It spun the top as it went in. "I cast you out, Devil. This beast of burden," she gestured dramatically to the cat, "has slain you, and your days of darkening the doorsteps of the witless are over."

"I really do hate you," I told her.

"I know." She bowed to me with an exaggerated flourish. "And I'm okay with that." She gave the cat a scritch on the ear. "What will you name him?"

"I can't keep him. Look at him. He's too friendly not to belong to someone else."

"He belongs to someone, all right." Linda pointed at me. "You, *Kleinkind*. He belongs to you."

I picked up the furball, and he let me hold him like a baby. His purring kicked up a notch as I rubbed his belly. "I would have remembered adopting this adorable chonky-chonky."

"As it is with his kind, he picked you." The gnome looked bewildered. "Though, I've never heard of a witch being chosen so quickly. Especially one that has come to the tru-craft so late in life."

"Hey," I said. "Didn't you say you were a couple of centuries-old? Forty-three is not that late."

"Not for a gnome, but for a witch, it's middle-aged." Linda hopped up on a chair. She was surprisingly fast and light on her feet. "Most witches get activated in their late teens and early twenties. The fact that your power has remained latent until now is a mystery. Maybe he's just been waiting for you."

"Or," I countered. "You, the cat, and everything else that's happened to me since yesterday is a manifestation of a depressive psychosis."

Linda snorted. "Okay, Randle."

I recognized the reference from *One Flew Over the Cuckoo's Nest*. The movie starring Jack Nicholson came out sometime in the seventies, several years before I was born. "Does that make you Nurse Ratched?"

My doorbell rang then I heard my sister Rose yell from the living room, "Iris, are you up?"

I went deer in the headlights as she strolled into the kitchen. "There you are." My younger sister had on a cream and gold patterned maxi dress. The top was cut tank-top style and showed off her muscular arms, courtesy of years of cross-fit training.

I gave her a half-hearted wave. "Oh, hey, Rose. I was going to call you today..."

"Sure you were," she said as she poured herself a cup of coffee. Her sandy blonde hair was straight as a pin, and she wore it down past her shoulders. My parents had adopted Rose three years after me, and even as a child, she had been serious and sober in her demeanor. She joined me at the table then looked down at the chair where Linda was standing. I almost *eeped* as Rose lifted her off the chair and set her on the counter. "Why is the garden gnome in the kitchen?"

Linda had gone stony. Of course, she had, I told myself. Linda was always stone.

"I, uhm, there was a—" I snapped my fingers. "She got knocked over outside, so I cleaned her up."

Rose gave me a worried glance. "Are you sure you're okay, Iris?"

"Oh, fine. Absolutely, terrific." Why didn't I just tell Rose I'd been drugged? After all, she'd find out when I hired Don to be my lawyer to take the case. On top of that, Rose was great at problem-solving. Hell, she'd not only arrange my drug testing and the lawsuit, but she'd also coordinate the police search for whoever supplied the drugs to the old lady in the first place. I opened my mouth to tell her what had happened, only I couldn't. Instead, I said, "You know. Just having an off morning."

"I can imagine." She nodded her head sympathetically. "Ooo!" she got up from her seat. "What's that?"

I looked under the table. The cat, who I'd forgotten about once my sister arrived and Linda went inanimate, was winding his way in and around Rose's legs.

"Oh, my gosh," she gushed. "Did you get a cat?"

"Uhm, sort of." I grimaced. "He showed up."

"When?"

"Last night, I think."

She picked him up to get a better look. "He's tiny but solid. Someone's been feeding him well. Are you sure he's a stray?"

"I'm not sure of anything." And I was talking about more than the cat.

"You should see if he's chipped."

"Yeah, that was on my to-do list." Along with getting drug tested and possibly checking myself into a psychiatric facility.

"Look at his little bobbed tail. Oh," her blue eyes brightened, "what if he's part bobcat, or all bobcat and just a runt."

"Sure." I snorted a laugh. "He's a bobcat."

Rose smiled. "What's his name? I mean, if you're keeping him, he needs a name, right?"

"Bob," I said. "Why not?"

Rose laughed, and it was nice to see my sister relax for a moment. "Hi there, Bob," she said to the cat as she continued to scratch his belly. "Welcome to the family."

"If he's not chipped," I added.

Rose nodded. "Of course."

"How are Drake and Dustin?" Drake and Dustin were Rose's Irish twins. They'd been born ten months and eleven days apart, with Drake being the oldest. Even so, Dustin, like his mother, was the more serious-minded of the two boys.

"They're good. I can't believe Drake is starting high school next year. I think he's both excited and terrified about becoming a freshman."

"Michael will look out for him."

Rose smiled. "There are perks to having a star athlete as a cousin. How is Michael holding up?"

"Oh, you know." I shrugged. "He has his good days and bad days. Evan moving in with Adam has thrown him off balance, but I'm sure he'll right himself soon enough."

My sister nodded sympathetically. "Absolutely. He's a strong kid. Change is hard, but he'll get through it. Especially with you in his corner."

I laughed. I couldn't even keep my own sanity in check. How in the world was I going to help my son? "I'd love to get to a point where I didn't love Evan anymore. At least then, I could stop hating him for throwing our marriage in the trash."

Rose put Bob down then sat in Linda's chair. She put her hand on top of mine. "Why don't you let me hate him for you? That will free up your emotions for better uses."

"I don't think it works that way. I wish it did."

"Did Marigold introduce you to her friend?"

"You mean Professor Snape?"

"Oh, Marigold made it out like he was gorgeous. Was he really awful?"

"No," I admitted. "Marigold wasn't wrong. He's very handsome."

"Then what's the problem? Was he rude?"

"No. Not rude."

"So tell me why you aren't interested."

"Maybe because I just signed my divorce papers two days ago." My tone bristled with annoyance.

"It's been over a year since Evan moved out and moved on. Don't you think it's time for you to do the same?"

I stood up and dumped my coffee in the sink. "Maybe I'll stay single until I die a happy old spinster," I said. "And I'm done having this conversation." I glanced at Linda, who was still in the same solid pose, wishing she was alive and calling me floppy tits again. "I'll be ready when I'm ready, and until then, I don't need you or Marigold trying to set me up with anyone."

"We love you, is all," Rose said, unperturbed. Thank heavens she didn't get butt hurt easily. "But if you want us to back off, then that's exactly what we'll do."

"We will, huh?"

Rose stood up as I walked over to her, and we hugged. "We will," she agreed.

"I'm sorry," I told her. "Maybe wait on the matchmaking

until I have at least a week under my divorce."

"You got it." She squeezed me tighter. "I have to get home. I promised the boys I'd take them to the pool today."

"Is that open already?" The community pool had been around since we were kids, and when Michael was little, I loved taking him there and watching him play.

"Last weekend." Rose let me go. "You and Michael come over for dinner Sunday night, okay?"

It wasn't as if I had better plans. I smiled. "I'll tell Michael to keep his calendar open."

My phone rang. The number came up as unknown.

"You going to get that?" Rose asked.

"It's probably a robocall or a scammer."

Her brow creased. "At seven o'clock in the morning? Ambitious."

I ignored the rings as I said my goodbyes to Rose. When I went back into my kitchen, Linda the gnome was gone, Bob the Cat was chasing a dryer sheet around the tiled floor, and my cell phone had one new message. Most robocalls didn't leave voicemails.

I tapped the icon to listen to messages and put my phone on speaker as I rinsed my coffee cup and wiped it out.

I recognized the smooth, sexy voice of Marigold's occult professor. "This is Keir Quinn. I'm just checking in to see when you're available to meet and discuss my book. I'm free this afternoon if you have the time. You have my number."

I could see the appeal of the man. Honestly, if I were less raw from getting my heart torn out, I might be hot for teacher. But right now, I had bigger fish to fry. Instead of calling Keir back, I called my brother about scheduling a rapid drug test.

# CHAPTER 8

I'D USED RUBBER CLEANING GLOVES TO WRAP CLING FILM around the book and tucked it away in the box it came in. I double-taped the top and shoved it in my closet. I drove to the hospital after and spent over an hour waiting for the lab to call me back. It only took a few minutes to pee in a cup and have my blood drawn—a quick in and out. The nurse told me it would take twenty-four hours to get the results.

My brother had encouraged me to contact the police. I told him I would if the lab found anything. There was no sense filing a crime report if I couldn't prove something had been done to me.

Bob was sitting on the front porch when I got home. I didn't know how he'd gotten out of the house. By the same token, I'd had no idea how he'd gotten inside the night before. He made some adorable, trill-like noises as I dug the house keys out of my purse.

"Hey, boy." I unlocked the door and opened it. "Let me

call one of the vets here in town, and we'll take care of you next."

Instead of going in, the cat took off like a shot around the house.

"Hey, come back!" Damn it, Bob. I threw my purse in the door then took off after him. My small backyard garden was surrounded by a privacy fence. I didn't see Bob, but there were spaces under the base where he could have tunneled in. I flung the gate open.

"Bo—" A clod of dirt and grass smacked me in my open mouth. I spit out what I could, then used the bottom of my T-shirt to get the mud off my tongue. Another dirt clod pelted me in the chest, then another smacked my ear. I danced around, scouring the garden for the source of the projectiles. My eyes widened as I found my target.

Linda.

My lip curled into a snarl as I clenched my fists and glared at the miniature bane of my existence. I was reasonably confident that whatever drug had been in my system was out. After all, I'd spent almost two hours away from the house without a single hallucination. So, why was that stupid gnome alive and taking potshots at me. "What the actual fuck, Linda?"

Linda, who was standing on my bench now, had another dirt clod in her hand. "I'm teaching you a valuable lesson, *Kleinkind*."

"And just what lesson would that be?"

She reared back and let loose with another zinger.

I dropped to the ground, and the clot hit the fence with a thud. "That one had a rock in it, Linda. You could've really hurt me."

The gnome crossed her arms and gave me a satisfied nod. "You're a slow learner, but at least you can be taught."

"How am I slow?"

"It took you getting hit three times before you ducked." She gave me a gotcha wink. "But you eventually got there."

"That was the lesson? To duck?" I couldn't keep the incredulity out of my tone.

"Failure is the greatest teacher," she said. "The important part is that you keep going until you get it right."

"What kind of evil Yoda bullshit is this, Linda?"

"Unlike Yoda," she countered. "I write all my own material."

I shook the dirt from my shirt and plucked a blade of grass from my hair. "Is there a point to all this?"

A chirping noise drew my attention. "Oh!" My heart did a backflip. "Isn't he adorable?" Bob was on his back near the yarrow plant, playing with ladybugs. "I love him so much."

"He's designed for you to love him, you dolt." Linda had a flair for words.

"I bet you won all kinds of popularity contests in high school."

"Do I look human to you?"

"Two arms, two legs, ten fingers and toes, no third eyes or extra nostrils. I mean, other than your height, you look pretty human to me."

"I have twelve toes," she said. "And I'm over two hundred years old."

"So, no prom."

Linda chucked a rock at me. It hit just above my right knee.

"Ow." I rubbed the spot. "That really stings."

She rolled her eyes. "One of these days, you'll move out of the way, *Kleinkind*."

"What does that mean? I know you're insulting me, but I'm just not sure how."

"Like I said before, look it up."

"I will." My phone was in my purse, and I'd thrown my purse in the house. "Once I get my cell phone."

She stuck her tongue out at me.

"Can you keep an eye on Bob? I need to make an appointment with the pet clinic to see if he belongs to someone else."

"You can't do that," Linda said.

"And why not?"

"Two reasons. Bob belongs to you."

"I think that reason falls under wishful thinking. I've only just met Bob, and he might have owners who are very worried about him. What's reason number two?"

"Bob has two hearts and no butthole."

"Excuse me?"

"Clean the cotton out of your ears."

"More like dirt," I said. "That you put there, by the way. I actually heard you, but I am super confused."

"It's simple, *wunderkind*. Kind of like you. Bob had two hearts. One for his life and one for yours. And no butthole."

"How does he poop?"

"He doesn't. Bob doesn't eat, so he doesn't need to poop."

"But he has balls."

"Of course, he does. Procreation is an essential function for imps. It's not like there's a familiar factory stamping them out down an assembly line. And, imps do drink, so the fluid has to leave their body somewhere."

"Like milk and water?"

Linda snorted. "Like whiskey and rye." She shook her head at my worried frown. "But only on special occasions."

"Like when they get to procreate?"

"See, I told you. Slow learner, but you get there eventually."

"Bob may not have an asshole, but you are one."

"Believe you me, *Kleinkind*, when a *Hexenmeister* comes for you—and one will—you'll be glad you have an asshole on your side."

"I find that hard to believe." Note to self: look up *Kleinkind* and *Hexenmeister*. And imps and gnomes. I shook my head at Bob. No butthole. Ouch. "Poor baby."

"Again," Linda said. "He doesn't eat."

Bob, in complete defiance of the grouchy gnome, chomped on a ladybug. "Eww, Bob. No."

"He'll throw it up later," Linda assured me.

I grimaced at the idea of a ladybug hairball. "Terrific." I narrowed my gaze on the gnome. "So, this is really happening, isn't it? You, Bob, the bossy blonde in the bathrobe..."

Linda laughed. "That description fits Bogmall as well as any I've heard. She is a bossy bitch."

"I said blonde."

Linda shrugged. "Tomatoes potatoes."

"But all real."

"Slow, but—"

"I get there." I rolled my eyes. "And I supposedly have some superpowers."

"Well, you can't leap tall buildings in a single bound or

dodge bullets." She gave me a meaningful stare. "You can't even dodge rocks. But, yes, you are brimming with magic."

"Prove it." I wiggled my fingers. "Teach me a spell or something."

"You should understand the fundamentals of terra-craft before doing actual spells."

"Blah, blah, Obe-Wonky-Gnomie. If the force is so strong in me. I should be able to do something with it."

"You watch entirely too much Star Wars."

"I like science fiction. It has gotten me through a rough time of late."

She crossed her arms over her chest and tapped a winklepicker on a paving stone. After a few moments, she nodded. "Fine. I think I can teach you a spell that won't end up with you demolishing your house."

A jolt of fear ran through me. "Is that a possibility?"

She looked contemplative, then said, "We're probably fine."

I shuffled nervously. "What do I do?"

"First, what was your intention?"

"I don't know."

"The Fade or the Bright. Which one?"

"My crystal went gray," I told her.

"That's...unusual." Linda didn't say it like it was a good thing.

"What does gray mean?"

"It means your magic is divided between Fade and Bright." She steepled her fingers. "That's a recipe for disaster."

I puckered my butt cheeks. "Solar flares out my ass kind of disaster?"

"Eh…I'll have to do a little research." Linda waved her hand at me. "But let's not focus on that right now."

"Is it normal to have both?"

"Honestly, you're a first for me, but I haven't been around as long as some of the gnomes in my donsy."

"So, in two hundred years, you've never met anyone who carried both the Fade and the Bright?"

"Nope." She hopped down from the bench and jogged over to me. Next, she offered me a small piece of gravel.

"What am I supposed to do with this?"

"I want you to hold the pebble in your hand and search it with your mind to find any cracks or fissures, and when you find them, I want you to concentrate on stretching them open."

"Then what?"

"Hopefully, the rock will fall apart in your palm."

"And if nothing happens?"

"We'll try until something does happen."

"Got it," I said, taking the stone. "Slow to learn, but I eventually get there."

I held the piece of pea gravel in my hand and tried to think what a fissure would even look like. The community pool popped into my head. It had a seam along the center that divided the shallow end from the deep end. It had been a milestone marker for me when I was young. The day I could swim past it without being afraid of drowning made me feel so grown up. I'd been eleven at the time. I thought about what that seam had felt like as I rotated the rock in my hand, feeling for cracks, crevices, any weak spots.

"Are you focused?" Linda asked.

I nodded. "Yes."

"Good. Now give your spell the nudge it needs with words."

"What words? I don't know any magic words."

"The spell will know what you want. It will read your thoughts."

"Then why do I have to say them at all?"

"I didn't write the rulebook, *Kleinkind*. Stop asking so many damn questions and do as I say."

"Fine." I sighed. "I'm not a spontaneous writer, so this is going to be terrible." Cracks, crevices, seams. This felt ridiculous, but I did as Linda instructed. "Crevices and cracks won't break no backs but stretch them wide, and they will divide."

A surge of energy rushed through me and away as if I were sending it out into the world. Eagerly, I opened my hand. The rock was intact. "I did something wrong." *Or, magic isn't real, bonehead.* "But it felt like something happened."

Linda had gone three shades paler. "Something definitely happened."

I heard the wail of sirens in the distance. It sounds like the whole Southill EMS was being rolled out.

"Oh, crap. Please don't tell me I broke the mountain."

"Not the mountain," a man said. I whipped around and saw Keir Quinn standing in front of my gate. "But you did drain the public pool."

"Hello, Quinn," Linda said. "I was wondering when you would show up."

# CHAPTER 9

KEIR'S DARK HAIR FLOATED AWAY FROM HIS HEAD, drifting out like curls of smoke. "I have sealed the crack." His voice vibrated with intensity. "For now." He turned his glittering iron gaze on the gnome. "Wroxishighomas Lupesabeinfeltchner."

"Gesundheit," I said as I tried to process what he'd just said about the pool. The sirens stopped. That was a good sign, right? "How do you know something happened at the pool? And why are you at my house? Even better question, how do you know where I live?" If Marigold gave him my address, I was going to kill her.

Linda, who had recovered some of her color, glared at the man. "I go by Linda, now," the gnome told him.

Keir glared back. "Why are you trying to destroy Southill, Earth guardian?"

"I'm not," Linda protested. "That was all the girl."

Girl? She couldn't mean me. "I didn't do anything." I held out the intact piece of gravel. "I couldn't even break a rock."

Keir frowned. "Because you broke a fifty-foot-wide piece of concrete instead."

I shook my head. "That can't be true."

Linda pelted me with another clod. "Please tell me you weren't focusing your energy on a pool filled with humans, *Kleinkind.*"

"I wasn't—" Only, I had been. I'd been thinking about my triumphant swim from the kiddie side into the deep waters of adulthood. And the pool had been on my mind because of... "Oh, no. Rose."

I shouldered my way past Keir and ran around the house to the front door. I flung it open, scrambling for my purse.

"What's wrong?" Keir asked. "Can I help?"

"My sister and her kids. Oh, no, no, no." Please let them be safe. I tapped the screen over her number. After four rings, the call went to voicemail.

*This is Rose. You know what to do at the beep.*

I hung up and hit her number again.

*This is Rose. You know what to do at the beep.*

"Please, please, Rose, answer the damn phone." Once more, the call went to voicemail. Dread and fear burned through my lungs. I squatted on my thighs, my lungs burning as I struggled to breathe.

Keir knelt beside me. "Rose is the youngest sister, right?" He put his hand on my back. The heat of his palm seeped into my skin. The warmth eased some of my anxiety to the point where I could speak.

"She took the boys to the pool today." I hiccupped as I met his gaze. "What if I've killed her? What if I've killed her family?"

Linda stood on the other side of me. She and Keir exchanged a look that made me worry even more.

The gnome shrugged. "Most witches can barely make dust levitate." There was a hint of pride in her voice.

Keir's voice was soft and soothing but with a hint of reprimand. "This is why you don't start with spells."

It dawned on me that this paranormal professor knew a little too much about what was happening with me. The timing of him showing up at my house, or in my life, for that matter, wasn't a coincidence. The realization frightened me, but not enough to override my concern for my sister and her kids.

I grabbed my keys and pushed myself up to a stand. My legs felt almost boneless as I swayed. Keir's hands dipped down, encircled my waist, and braced me up.

"Hang in there." His breath was silky against my neck, sending a shiver down my spine. "It's going to be all right."

"You can't know that." What would Don do if something happened to Rose? What would either of them do if the boys were hurt or worse? The devastation would be too much to bear. "I have to go. I have to find Rose." I pushed away from Keir and stumbled to the door.

The phone, still gripped in my hand, rang. My knees buckled, and I went down hard on them. Rose. It was Rose. I fumbled to answer and hung up instead. "Son of a bitch," I hissed as I called her back. Another beep told me I had an incoming call.

Keir gently took the phone, ended my call out, and accepted Rose's call in. He handed it back to me.

"Hello," I said quickly. "Rose, are you there?"

"Iris!" She didn't sound hurt, angry, or devastated. On the

contrary, Rose seemed exhilarated. "You're not going to believe what happened."

"Are you okay?"

"Yes, sorry," she said. "My heart is thumping so loud right now I can barely think."

Blood rushed back to my limbs, freeing my legs to move. "What happened?"

"You know how I told you this morning that I was taking the boys to the pool?"

"Yes, I recall," I said. It was a warm day, but I was shivering.

"I think we had an earthquake. The concrete shook, and the pool cracked open about an inch. It was enough to break the drain lines, the filters, and the pipes. Water is spraying everywhere!"

"That's terrible."

"It's so cool," I heard Drake say. "You should see it, Aunt Iris."

"You boys stay right next to me," Rose told her sons before returning to the conversation. "Anyhow, the lifeguards were able to get everyone out, but, wowza, the shaking knocked down a powerline. Sparks were flying for a few seconds before the transformer fritzed and the power went out. Firetrucks, the police, and two ambulances are here, but no one was injured, thankfully. Still, it's totally nuts. Did you know we had fault lines through our town? I mean, that's what I heard one of the first responders say. Don said he didn't feel a thing at the office. Gosh, I hope the house is still standing when I get home. You only live about a mile from here. Did you feel it at your place?"

"Maybe." Tears blurred my vision as I sagged with relief. "I'm not sure."

No one had been hurt. No one died.

"Iris?" Rose asked. "Are you okay?"

"Now that I know you're all right." I wiped my eyes. "I'm just glad you and the boys are safe."

"I'm glad you're safe, too," she said. "Are you sure you're okay? You seemed off this morning."

"I'm fine. Tell the boys I'll take them for ice cream next week. Love you." I disconnected the call before Rose could ask any more questions.

"She's okay?" Keir asked.

"Yes, she and the kids are fine." I stared at him. "But you knew. You said it would be all right."

Linda clapped her hands together. "Excellent. No harm, no foul."

If laser beam eyeballs had been one of my superpowers, Linda would have been cut in half by my glare. "You're kidding, right?"

"Next time, you'll improve your aim."

"Next time?" My voice raised an octave. "Next time? There's not going to be a next time, Linda." I might be slow, but my mama hadn't raised an idiot." I rounded on Keir as the fear for Rose abated, and my suspicion and anger returned. "And you..." I shook my finger at him. "You, son-of-a-bitch." The fact that he was here, that he was talking to Linda, and that he knew magic existed might not tell me everything I needed to know, but it told me a lot. "You manipulated my sister, didn't you? You used her to get me to that auction."

He didn't deny it.

"You're the reason I bid on the box of toxic books." Even if they hadn't been drugged, the tomes had done me nothing but harm.

Keir met my gaze. The light gray color of his eyes had turned to a darker pewter tone. "I'm not the reason you found the grimoires. I only help facilitate the opportunity. It was your ancestor's magic that drew you to them as I hoped they would."

"I don't care about ancestors or magic. This is not me. Whatever you and the gnome have done to me, I want you to take it back."

Linda hissed. "Don't say that. Don't ever say that."

Keir pursed his lips. His brow furrowed in consternation. "You're a witch, Iris. A descendant of the Islandmagee witches. This would have been easier had you been raised by your own kind, but it doesn't negate the fact that their magic is in your DNA, and it was going to manifest one way or another."

I didn't know what to say. Was Keir telling me the truth, or was he telling me what he thought I needed to hear to get on board with whatever plan he and the gnome had for me? God, I sounded mad.

Keir turned his hand over, palm up, and setting at the center was a gray shard—the one from my dream. "Take your focus. You left it behind at the choosing."

A star-shaped scar was on his wrist. I recognized it from my woodsy adventure the night before. "You." He'd been the first person the blonde woman with the scars on her face had ordered to demonstrate what I was supposed to do. His crystal had turned white. "You were one of the robed minions."

"Minion sounds about right." Linda chuckled.

"I'm not a minion."

"Is the blonde your leader?"

"Of sorts," he admitted.

"And you do what she says?"

He pursed his lips then said, "Yes."

I nodded. "You're a total minion."

"Whatever you think of me, I am here to help you, Iris. If you don't master your magic, you will be in great danger."

"I'm not a witch," I said petulantly.

Linda made an "eh" sound. "The minion's not wrong. You are a witch."

I stared at Keir. "Are you a witch, too? Or a warlock? Whatever male witches are called."

"Male witches are called witches, but no, I'm not one. My magic doesn't involve any spellwork. I'm a druid."

"And then some," Linda said. "You're more than that, Keir Quinn."

"I am what I am," he said cryptically. "But that is not for you to say."

I'd seen enough movies and read enough books to know what druids were. At least in theory, but other than building Stonehenge and someone eating a fish of knowledge, I was pretty clueless to what a druid actually did. "What kind of magic do you have?"

"I'm a prognosticator."

I knew what the word meant—a prognosticator was someone who foretells the future. "So, you're a seer? Is that why you knew my sister would be all right?"

"Not exactly. I can't see everyone's future. Druids are committed to finding witches and guiding them."

"I bet that came in handy during the Salem Witch Trials."

The corner of his lip curled up in a half-smile. "I wasn't alive during that time."

I glanced at Linda. She waved her hands. "I'm only two hundred. That crap happened long before me."

Keir knelt down beside me, his lithe frame graceful and his movement effortless. His expression softened as he reached out as if he might touch my cheek. He stopped just inches short and let his hand drop. "Even if I had been alive, Iris Everlee, I would have never used my gift to harm your kind."

He'd taken the crystal, and it had turned a milky white. "Is that because you're Bright?"

Keir chuckled. "I like to think I'm fairly bright."

"You know what I mean." I elbowed his thigh.

He wobbled, grinning as he righted himself. "Yes, I do know what you mean. My field of magic follows the Bright path." When Keir Quinn smiled, it was as if the whole world lit up with energy. Maybe that's what it meant to be on the Bright path. The gray in his eyes began to sparkle as if someone had strung my garden fairy lights behind his irises.

"How are you doing that?"

He held out his hand to me. "There's so much you need to learn, Iris. So much I want to teach you."

I melted at his words. His wide, firm lips were so close. How easy it would be to "accidentally" fall onto them with my own lips. "You have such a nice face," I said.

Keir caressed my cheek. "I like your face too."

A dirt clod smacked me in the temple. I whipped my glare at Linda. "None of that," she said.

Where in the world had she found a handful of dirt in the house? Did she carry the stuff in her pockets?

Linda snapped and pointed out the front door.

"Crap." The front door was still open, and I saw Michael exiting the passenger side of his father's car. "Not today," I croaked as I got up from the floor. I had to pull myself together. "My son is here."

"Mom?" Michael's pace quickened. "Did you fall?" He was at my elbow, helping me to my feet.

"I tripped, but I'm good." I dusted the knees of my yoga pants. "I thought you were riding with Doug?"

"Dad wants to talk to you." Michael gave Keir a funny look. "Who's this?"

Keir answered. "I'm a friend of your Aunt Marigold. I work at the college with her. I just hired your mom to do some freelance editing for me."

Michael, who I'm sure stopped listening after "Aunt Marigold," grunted. "Cool." He loped past us then stopped. "Why is the garden gnome on the living room floor?"

# CHAPTER 10

IN THE TWENTY-SOMETHING YEARS THAT I'D KNOWN EVAN Callahan, there was one thing that never changed—the man was still as handsome as ever. Even worse, I think he'd gotten better looking with age. His curly blonde hair and deep dimples were like salt in the wound.

I still had so many questions for Keir, but I couldn't blow off my ex. Not in front of Michael. I'd worked tirelessly this past year to make this divorce as amicable as possible. Evan hadn't fought for custody, and he'd given up his half of the house. Because of that, I hadn't asked for alimony, only child support. My editing job paid the bills. Since my home was paid for, the only expenses I had were utilities, groceries, and whatever Michael needed.

As Evan sauntered up the sidewalk toward the front door, I turned to Keir. "Can we talk later?"

Keir's fingertips casually brushed the back of my hand. "I have a house north of town. I'll text you the address."

As he left, I could still feel the lingering sensation of his skin on mine. When he passed Evan, they gave each other the 'sup nod. I rolled my eyes. Men. "Come on, Linda." I picked up the gnome and carried her into the kitchen with Evan on my heels.

"Hey, Iris," he said. He rarely made eye contact with me anymore. I guess I couldn't blame him. If I'd cheated on him and got caught, I would have moved to a vacant island in some far-off land so that I would never have to show my dishonest, vow-breaking face to anyone ever again.

Of course, that was just me.

I set Linda down on the counter but turned her toward the wall as my little FU to the sarcastic gnome. "I signed the papers two days ago, Evan. All done. Don filed them at the courthouse, so we are officially no longer married."

"Uhm, great." He shuffled his loafered feet alongside the stone tile. "I wanted to talk to you before I told Michael..."

I narrowed my gaze. "Told Michael what?"

"Adam and I are..." He was so hesitant, I thought it could only be one thing.

"Getting married?"

Evan's blue eyes got big. A mixture of shock and surprise. "No. I mean, we've bandied it about, but no."

"Then what? Just spit it out, Evan."

"We're thinking about moving."

"Okay." I knew he was renting an apartment right now. "Are you buying a house?" Mr. Federer's place, one block over from my house, had a for sale sign on the lawn. For all that was sacred, I pleaded with the universe that he wasn't trying to move him and his boyfriend into the neighborhood.

"Yes, I mean, we'd like to buy a house." Evan wiggled his

nose. Something he did when he was nervous. Something I used to think was cute. "In St. Louis."

"St. Louis? You are really trying to erase your past, huh? I can see why you don't want to talk to Michael about this."

He tried to put a consoling hand on my arm, but I moved out of his reach. "I'm sorry, Iris. I hate that I keep hurting you. That I keep hurting our son. Adam's been offered a coaching job at a private school there. I've put out feelers for a teaching position at several universities. Wouldn't your life be easier if I left town? Wouldn't Michaels?"

Hadn't I just been wishing he'd have gone off to a deserted island? Still, it hurt thinking about what this news would do to Michael. "You can't just leave our son like this."

"He's going into his senior year. Soon he'll be off to college."

"Adam wants to take the job, doesn't he?"

"It's almost twice as much money as he makes now, and the athletic program is competitive."

Tears welled in my eyes, and I hated myself for crying. But the tears weren't for me. If Evan moved, I worried what it would do to Michael. It would be like losing his dad all over again.

He put his arms around me. "I'm sorry, Iris. I'm so sorry." I knew he wasn't talking about moving. He'd apologized a million times since the night I found out about him and Adam. This was a million and one.

I clenched my fist as anger welled inside me as I wished for thicker skin. Something so impenetrable, nothing could get past it to hurt me. I had never thought of myself as weak but losing Evan had turned me into a woman I couldn't stand. A woman I didn't want to live with anymore. I would be strong. A pillar for my son, and for him, I would weather every storm.

"Let me go, Evan." My voice was cold even to my own ears. "I don't care what you do anymore. Stay, move, get married. What you do is no longer my business. You no longer have any kind of hold on me." A burst of power jolted from my core and out my chest. Evan tore away from me, his head smacking the refrigerator.

The violence of it snapped me out of my rage. "Oh my god, Evan. Are you okay?"

"Christ, Iris. You could've given me a concussion." He rubbed the back of his head. "Have you been doing cross-fit with Rose?"

"I didn't—" I rubbed my arms to dissipate the residual energy rippling across my skin. "I didn't mean to. I guess I'm not as evolved as I thought." I chuckled so I wouldn't cry anymore.

"What's that on your hand?" he asked.

I looked where he had pointed. There was a gray patch about the size of a quarter just below my wrist on my left hand. I touched it. It felt like...bark. What the hell? I'd wished for tougher skin. Had I done this to myself? This and a dozen more questions were for Linda and not for my ex. "You should go, Evan. You've said what you came to say. When you and Adam decide what you're going to do, we can sit down with Michael."

"But your hand."

"Is also not your problem." I leaned on the counter and tucked my bark-skinned hand behind my back.

Evan sneezed. He glanced around the kitchen. He sneezed violently this time, and his eyes started watering.

Bob jumped up on the counter next to Linda and growled. It made me smile. Crazy imp. He definitely knew how to read a mood.

"When did you get a cat?" He sneezed a couple more times. "I've got to go before my eyes swell shut."

"Good idea. You should get you some Benadryl." I ran my hand down Bob's back as Evan fled the kitchen.

When he was out of the house, Linda said, "Don't let the door hit ya, where the good lord Vidar split ya." She sat down on the counter, swinging her legs off the edge. "I never did like him."

I sighed wistfully. "I did." I put my barky hand in front of Linda. "What is this, and how do I get rid of it?"

"It looks like ironbark." She grabbed my hand and turned it over. There was another spot on my forearm. "This isn't good."

It reminded me of my dad's eczema. "Do you think a steroid cream might help?"

"This isn't something that any modern medicine can fix, *Leibling*. You've cast a spell, and now you have to uncast it."

"I did not." Only, I knew I had. I'd wished to be strong enough to break Evan's hold, and my powers had literally thrown him away from me. But I hadn't asked for skin covered in bark. "Could this be a side effect of magic?"

"All magic has a cost, but it's usually little things, like a single hair falling out or a nail breaking. I've never seen it do this."

"How do I reverse a spell?"

"Your terra-craft is too unpredictable right now. Your sister wasn't wrong. There are fault lines in this mountain. I'm not saying you'll tear the mountain down, but..." She spread her hands out. "The only way you can fix this is by doing the work to master earth magic. Once it starts, you can't stop it."

I recalled the inscription, *Once it's begun, it cannot be undone.* I didn't understand it then, but I did now.

"Any good news?" I asked hopefully.

She held up a finger and waved it at me. "There's only bad news."

"I hate you, Linda."

"I know, *Kleinkind.*" She stroked her beard. "Unfortunately, your magic is more powerful and unpredictable than I expected. I fear if you don't learn to control it soon, you will not survive the transition. The truth is, not all witches survive going from the spark to full transition. There are only two choices, embrace the tru-craft or die trying."

My throat felt thick as I swallowed back my fear. "How much time do I have?"

She gave me a solemn look. "You picked a terrible time to spark. There is a lunar eclipse on the twenty-sixth of this month. The combination of the super moon and the eclipse will magnify all magic. Your power is already strong, and your lack of control will cause you to..." She produced a pea-sized pebble in her hand, pulverized it between her fingertips, then blew the dust in my face.

"Got it. Dust in the wind." I'd gotten a notice on my weather app about the lunar eclipse. It was a rare supermoon event, and when I'd read about it, it had sounded pretty cool. Now, it sounded terrifying. "That's in four days. I've known magic is real for like a minute, and now I have to pull off mastering this terra-craft stuff in four friggin' days? How many times have you told me I'm a slow learner? I'm not going to make it."

"You'll make it, *Leibling*," Linda said. "I swear it." She leaped to the floor. "Just no spellwork for now. We'll stick to the basics of understanding how nature works."

"If you knew doing a spell was dangerous, why did you let me do it?"

"Because, as I said before, failure is often our greatest teacher."

"You knew I'd fail, then."

"Not so spectacularly, but yes." Linda cast a look over her shoulder at me as she walked through the wall. "But, I hoped you wouldn't."

My hero, Bob the Imp Cat, stood up and rubbed his body on my arm. I found it oddly calming. Then, he circled the counter and twitched his tail at me. My eyes widened. Linda was right. Bob didn't have a butthole. Which meant I wouldn't have to buy kitty litter or cat food. "You might just be perfect."

Bob meeped, a cute little sound of contentment, then yarked a hairball up next to my sink.

## CHAPTER 11

I'D USED BANDAGES FROM THE FIRST AID KIT TO COVER THE two bark-like areas on my wrist and arm. Michael came into the kitchen a few minutes later. He had been going to his friend Doug's house every afternoon this week, so Linda's lessons in supernatural horrors would have to wait until he was gone. Michael had showered and changed into shorts and a tank top. This was not his usual "hang" wear.

"Are you in for the day?"

"Yep."

"It's Friday. You don't have a hot date or something?"

"I'm playing the new Battle Call of the Wild Seven with Doug and Jake." Michael opened the fridge and freezer at the same time and scoured the shelves. "Are we out of orange juice?"

"Yeah, sorry. I'll go to the grocery store this afternoon. Do you want me to get some snacks for you and the guys?" I hadn't been food shopping this week, and Doug alone could pound down some grub. His words, not mine.

"For me," he said. "I'll take some tortilla chips, a couple cans of nacho cheese, and some stuff to make salsa."

"And the guys?" The bark on my wrist and forearm itched under the bandages.

"They're playing from home." He was still standing in the open doors. He knew it drove me nuts, but I tried hard not to take the bait. I didn't have the energy to fight with him.

I'll admit, the news that I wasn't going to have two more teenagers running around the house today relieved me. Don't get me wrong. I loved Michael's friends. They'd been as much a part of getting him through the last year with his sanity intact as I had. However, if they were playing together online, it meant that Michael's recent shower was probably going to be his last for the entire weekend. Those boys could get dug in when it came to a new Battle Call game. It also meant that I couldn't attend Linda's workshop on "how not to destroy my life with terra-craft." Since I only had a few days to Dust Day, I would have to figure out how to interact with the gnome-from-hell when Michael was home.

Michael pulled a nearly empty milk jug out then put it back as he casually asked, "What did Dad want?"

Ah, the real reason he was letting all the cold out of the fridge and freezer. Damn it. Why had Evan talked to me about his moving plans before he'd spoken to Michael? This wasn't a secret I wanted to keep from my kid, but I also didn't want to ruin his weekend by dropping the bomb on him that his father might or might not be moving to another state.

"You know your dad. It's always something." Why did it feel like I was constantly navigating Evan and Michael's relationship? Oh, because I was. Frankly, I didn't want to be in the middle of their stuff. Not anymore. As of two days ago, I wasn't married to Evan. I didn't have to keep acting like his wife, damn it. I was always the bad news giver. Evan didn't like conflict, which was why it took our son finding him in a compromising position before he admitted he'd fallen in love with someone else. If Evan didn't learn to communicate directly with our son, I was going to kill him.

The bark-skin burned, reminding me that even my thoughts could be dangerous. I would never wish Evan dead, so I mentally readjusted "kill him" with "kick his ass."

I walked to Michael and flicked the back of his head. "Close the refrigerator, kid."

He tried to smack my hand, but I jumped away.

"Hah, too slow." I danced back and forth on the balls of my feet and mimicked a right-left-right punch combo. "I float like a butterfly and sting like lemon juice in the eye."

"So lame," Michael said with a chuckle.

His laugh made me smile. "I'm going out this afternoon. I'll pick up some juice, and nacho fixin's on the way home. Do you want anything else?"

"We need milk. And you can get me some chocolate syrup if you want."

I pinched the peach fuzz on his jawline. "You got it."

"Uhm, did we get a cat?"

"Bob!" I picked up the imp and smooshed his whiskery face. He tilted his nose and bumped it on mine. The tension melted from my muscles, and my mood lightened. "This is Bob." And he was better than a Xanax.

Michael smiled and scratched the furry mood stabilizer between his short ears. "Hey, Bob."

Bob's purring kicked up a notch. "Oh, look. He loves you

already, Michael." I met my son's gaze. "You're pretty easy to love, though."

Michael rolled his eyes. "He's kind of dopey looking, but he's cool."

If Bob was offended by the dopey comment, he didn't show it. "Cool," I said. I gave him a quick hug. "Have fun today with your friends. I'll let you know when I get back with the food."

"Thanks, Mom."

"You got it, babe." Now, I had to break it to a cranky gnome that I was skipping class. Although, maybe I didn't need to skip it altogether. I went into the living room and rummaged in my purse until I found Keir Quinn's card. I had to talk to him sooner than later. With Michael being home for the rest of the day, sooner was the better option.

I went to the garden first. Linda was back in her place by my bench, giving it the old stony stare. I giggled. I couldn't believe I'd been blaming Michael this whole time for moving Linda, and she'd been doing it herself.

I sat down in my favorite spot. "Well, Mr. Miyagi, there will be no waxing on or waxing off today. The kid is home, and I don't want to have to explain any of this," I held up my bandaged arm, "to him. So, I'm headed to Keir Quinn's to get some answers. He seems to know a lot about me. About my ancestors." I sneered at the idea of my bio-family. It would be a lie to say I never thought about who they were, especially after I had Michael. Mainly because every time the pediatrician asked for family medical history, I had to leave it blank. Cripes. "Will Michael become a witch?"

"He already is," Linda said. "It's another reason you have to master your powers."

Her revelation exploded my brain. "Why didn't you tell me this before?"

"Before when? Before you knew what you were? You know, when you thought you were on drugs?

The gnome was right. I was just now coming to terms with the fact that magic was real. If she had told me Michael was a witch yesterday, I would have laughed in her face. "Don't get logical on me, Linda."

Her stony expression softened. "I don't say these things to make your life harder, *Leibling*. I say them because they are true. And the truth, as you well know, is the greatest gift."

"I don't know. A million dollars would be pretty awesome."

"What is money? Just paper to burn."

"Spoken like someone who doesn't have to pay bills."

Linda smirked. "That's also true." She walked over to me and placed her hand on my knee. "Take the grimoire," she said. "He can help you unlock its secrets."

"But it's empty."

"You better look, *Kleinkind*." She shook her head. "The only thing empty is your imagination."

"Just when I was starting to like you." The itching on my arm worsened. I lifted the bandage, and my stomach sank. The margins had gotten wider on the spot on my wrist. "It's getting worse." I checked my forearm. The dime-sized area was closer to a nickel now in size. "It's expanding."

"This is not good."

"Can you just..." I rubbed my fingers together on one hand. "Poof it like you did the rock earlier?" She'd turned it to dust without using any energy or having to say the words. "How did you do that, by the way? It was so effortless."

"I don't possess tru-craft. Only witches and *die Hexenmeister* can manipulate the elements with spellwork. I'm an earth spirit. Rocks, dirt, metals, and basically anything mineral-based are at my command. At least on a small scale. The way you walk through the air. The way the molecules move around you and out of your way so you can move unencumbered. That is the way with my kind." She disappeared into the grass and popped up almost instantly a few feet on the other side of the bench. The ground was undisturbed. "I know everything there is to know about terra, which is why I'm suited to instruct you in terra-craft."

"And the druid?"

"His story is for him to tell."

"You don't trust him?"

"It's not him, *Kleinkind*." She snorted, and a pebble shot out her nose. "I don't trust you. I see the way you looked at him. You just got rid of one distraction, and I'm not sure you can afford another. Your focus has to be the craft, and the craft is driven by emotion. If your *Laune*, your mood, is all over the place, your magic will be all over the place."

"You don't have to worry about me. I'm on a man break."

"Remember." Linda held up a finger, and surprisingly, not the middle one this time. "Your magic knows your heart. All the pretty words won't save you if the intention isn't there."

Michael opened the back door, and Linda froze in place.

"Hey, can you pick me up some Shock Cola?"

"That's terrible for you. It'll give you a—" I was going to say heart attack, but gah, words, intention, blah blah. "Pick a different drink."

His expression fell. "I'll just drink some iced coffee."

"Terrific," I told him.

"You going soon?" He rubbed his belly. "I'm getting hungry for nachos."

"There's ham in the fridge. Eat a sandwich. It'll hold you over until I get back." He closed the door, and Linda animated.

"Go," she said. "I will keep the boy safe."

"Is he in danger?"

"Mmm." Linda shrugged. "Your earlier explosion of energy might have attracted the wrong...kind of creatures."

Great. Now I had to worry about Michael's safety on top of not turning into magical dust. "Like who? And do I have to worry about Michael turning into dust too?"

"To a lesser degree, other Earth spirits like fairies, elves, and trolls. A troll showing up would be the worst of the three. Your terra-craft was powerful. Wild, yes. But some of the strongest I have ever felt. It's bound to attract some riff-raff." She adjusted her hat down over her ears. "As to Michael, he may never spark, but even if he does, we have years to teach him about the tru-craft before he might come into his magic."

We? Did this mean Linda was sticking around? I hadn't liked the gnome when she didn't talk. I liked her less now that she did. "What about other gnomes?"

She twisted her beard. "We don't fight amongst ourselves. But the Earth spirits are the least of my concern." She took a dramatic pause.

"Spit it out, Linda."

"I've already mentioned them a couple of times, but *die Hexenmeister* will be your most dangerous foes."

Crap. I still hadn't looked up *Hexenmeister*. "Do they hex people?"

Linda circled a finger at me. "Very close. *Die Hexenmeister* are kin to witches, and they can use the craft. However, unlike witches, a *Hexenmeister* isn't born with magic. They have to acquire it through sacrifice, and I'm not talking metaphorically. They sacrifice witches to siphon their magic. What do you think all the witch trials through the ages were about? Most of them were engineered by *die Hexenmeister* to gain magic without raising a fuss. Nowadays, they have to be more subtle about it." She raised her gaze to me. "And who better to acquire magic from than an untrained powerful witch on the verge of burning herself out."

I blinked. "When you put it that way..." I wanted to grab Michael, find the deepest, most secure vault I could find, and lock him in it. "Maybe I should stay home."

"Even if any of these elementals showed up, it wouldn't be tonight. I would feel their arrival, and so far, other than my brethren who are scattered throughout Southill Village, no other Earth spirits have arrived."

"And the *Hexenmeister*?"

"They're a little trickier. There is no way to detect one unless they use their borrowed power. But trust me, I can protect Michael if need be."

"You are less than two feet tall and have hands the size of my big toes."

Linda gave me a baleful glare. "Go to the druid. Talk to him. Then bring back food for your boy. Until then, take solace in the fact that I am watching over Michael."

"And Bob?"

She rolled her eyes so hard that all I saw were the whites. Eww.

"I will watch over the imp as well."

"Thanks, Linda. You're not so bad."

She put fisted hands on her hips, Superman-style. "And you are a dolt."

"I take it back. You're awful."

Linda narrowed her gaze at me. "Why are you still here?"

"I'm going, sheesh."

As I walked away, I felt a sharp sting of a rock bouncing off my right butt cheek. When I whipped around to confront Linda, she was back in her flowerbed, still as stone, and staring at my bench.

When I turned to walk away, I zigged sideways as another pebble zipped past me and bounced harmlessly off the side of my house. "Hah! Missed me, bitch."

My celebration ended when a large piece of sod smacked me in the back of my head.

"Do better," I heard Linda say as I scooted inside the house. "Learn faster."

I grabbed Keir's card to call him, but when I got to my phone, I saw I had a missed text. *22459 Bards Lane. Take the second gravel road. See you soon. KQ.*

Damn, he'd beaten me to the punch. Was it a coincidence? Or had he seen me coming with his gifts? Either way, it was time to go. I texted him back.

*On my way.*

The three dots that cycle on the screen when someone is writing a text kept starting and stopping. Finally, Keir wrote back. *I know.*

Brazen bastard.

# CHAPTER 12

Bard Lane was near the top of the mountain. By the time I arrived, I was seriously regretting the forty-four-ounce soda I'd guzzled in the half-hour trip. The gravel roads agitated my full bladder like Pop Rocks in a bottle of Mountain Dew. In other words, I was about to explode.

Finally, I pulled up and parked next to Keir Quinn's pale green Mini Cooper EV.

The property had a lot of tall white oak trees, a few red maples, and a variety of pines. But the vista of all views was a stunning waterfall that emptied into a stream behind Keir's tiny house.

I'd seen tiny homes on television, but I'd never seen one up close. Keir's looked like a tall shipping container with rustic wood siding and huge windows on the front and the back. I grabbed the grimoire from the passenger seat and hurried to the front door. I could easily see the waterfall from the door's window to the window in the back wall. I saw a couch, a sink, and full bookshelves under a steep staircase to a loft bed. The two things I couldn't see was Keir or a bathroom.

I danced around as my full bladder reminded me of my extra-large soda mistake.

I knocked on the wood trim. "Hello?" Where was he? He knew I was coming.

The door opened, and I stumbled back in surprise. I may or may not have peed myself a little. "Son of a bitch."

Keir smiled. "Hello to you, too."

"Where the heck did you come from?"

"Inside," he answered.

I wanted to argue because he had not appeared in front of the window before the door opened. But I had other dragons to slay. I crossed my legs and prayed to the bladder gods to give me urethral strength. "Do you have indoor plumbing or an outhouse?"

"I have a compost toilet under the loft."

"Oh, dear lord. Well, beggars can't be choosers." I pushed the book into his hands then wiggled past him, thankful I only had to go about four feet to a curtain under a wooden platform that I presumed was for his bed. "Get out," I yelled at Keir as I closed the curtain and yanked down my pants. "Get out now!"

The front door shut hard enough for me to hear it, and I let the flood go. And go. And goooooooo. My relief and my embarrassment were tied for top emotions. Linda had been worried for absolutely no reason. I'd pretty much guaranteed that even if Keir Quinn had ever seen me as a sexual prospect, it was over now.

I exited the toilet space and used what I assumed was the kitchen-slash-bathroom sink to wash my hands. There was a foot pump to run the water, and there was a bottle of no suds, environmentally friendly soap mounted on the wall. It took me a second, but I figured it out, then dried my hands.

I drew back the curtains and let out a breath I'd been holding that Keir had actually gone outside. He was standing in his backyard, appreciating the view. Now that I was less focused on my bodily functions, I let myself admire the view as well. The man wore a pair of jeans that fit snug on his well-formed ass, and even though his shoulders were narrow, I could see the definition of his muscles under the faded blue T-shirt he had on.

He looked over his shoulder—his eyes meeting mine through the glass—and grinned. "Can I come back in? Or do you want another minute to take in the scenery?"

My cheeks warmed. "You can come back in."

It took all of ten seconds for Keir to walk from the back of the house to the front.

"That's quite the workout," I said as he entered.

He arched a brow. "I hope you found the bathroom okay."

"It's easy to get lost in this mansion of yours, but I managed." I gestured to his couch, where he'd also left the grimoire. "Can I sit?"

"Sure," he said. "That's the living room and the guest bedroom. The sofa folds down into a day bed."

"Very efficient use of space." I sat down, and while I wouldn't call the cushions plush, they weren't uncomfortable. I glanced around the room. "Can I ask a question?"

"I like it up here. The mighty oaks can speak to me without the interference of electrical power lines and cell phone towers. Besides, I like living off the grid."

"How do you charge your car?"

"Solar panels in a clearing about two hundred yards up the road, and I charge my phone with the car."

"Where do you shower and stuff?" There hadn't been a shower in the curtained watershed bathroom.

"I built a solar shower near the falls. It collects rainwater, the sun heats it, and voila. If it doesn't rain, I just gather it from the creek there."

"So you have to walk out to the falls every day to shower?" I'll admit, the idea of Keir walking through the grass buck naked was not unappealing. "I couldn't live this way."

"When I am here, I am most myself, Iris. This place, for me, is like a spiritual awakening every time I step out of my vehicle."

"It's your church, huh?"

He chuckled. "Something like that."

"You said you came here for me. And you can see the future. My future, right?"

"Since you were born."

"Dude, I'm forty-three. You look younger than me."

"I'm forty-three, too," he said. "I was born on May 1st."

"Hey, that's my birthday." Or at least the one I'd been assigned. And I'd been abandoned when I was a few weeks old, so I had no birth certificate and no name. I'd been Baby Girl Doe until Grace and Randall Everlee took me in. They'd given me my birthdate as well.

"Yes." Keir took a book from the cramped shelves. "I was born two hours before you."

"But May 1st isn't even my real birthday."

He chuckled. "It is. I don't remember a lot from that day.

I was a newborn myself, but your birth has been with me since the moment you arrived."

"Wow, maybe my folks had been clairvoyant as well."

"Or your family's magic guided them."

I thought about Linda. Mom had insisted she go in my garden, and she made sure that Linda was sentimental enough to her that I would never get rid of the stony grump. Had the Magee coven, part of the clan who had named the peninsula in Ireland, had a hand in that as well?

Keir handed me the book. It was a textbook on Arthurian legends. "Did you know that Merlin the magician was a prognosticator? He could see Arthur even before he met him. What you won't read about in other books," he tapped the cover, "is that Merlin had been born two hours before Arthur, and he was born with the birthmark of a crown on his wrist. It was the symbol for Arthur Pendragon, the man whom Merlin would spend the rest of his life with." He smiled at me. "It was one of the greatest tales of love ever written."

"They were lovers?"

Keir shrugged. "Only Merlin and Arthur know, but I'm not talking about physical love. I'm talking about a bond that goes beyond that. It's a bond of friendship, companionship, and devotion. It's a bond that makes a person willing to give up their entire life to save the other."

"I do know what that's like."

His expression held the question.

"My son," I told him. "I knew the minute Michael was born I'd die for him. Even more, I'd kill for him."

The answer made Keir smile. "Yes, that's the bond I mean. It's the same for you and me."

I shifted uncomfortably in the seat. "Look, you seem like a nice guy and all, but I'm not sure I'd be willing to give up my life for you. I barely know you."

He laughed. "You don't understand. This kind of devotion is always one-sided for my ilk. I have been waiting for you to awaken since your birth. When it sparked last year, I came to find you."

"How did I spark? I don't understand. I haven't had any magical weirdness happen to me until I found the book."

"The spark happens for witches for a variety of reasons. Sometimes it's a happy event, sometimes it's a trauma. For some, there is no rhyme or reason. But it just means there is the potential, and that potential will try to find a way into this world.

I'd had a lot of bad stuff happen over the year. Maybe the divorce had been the reason. I hoped not. I didn't need one more reason to hate Evan. "So, I sparked, and you put me in the path of those books."

He raised his hand. "That was fate's doing, not mine."

"I think fate got a nudge." I tapped the book beside me. "You can see my future, right?"

He nodded. "Yes."

"Then tell me what happens next? Do I master this Earth crap in a few days or do I poof," I mimicked explosions with my hands, "and turn into magic dust?"

He took my hands. His fingers were warm, and my skin felt electrified under his touch. "I don't see one future, Iris. I see thousands of futures."

"All mine?"

"Every single one of them. Every possible choice you can make is constantly changing every outcome in any given situation. I can see the inevitability of certain situations playing out to a natural conclusion. Still, those conclusions are not written in stone. Some things are easier to predict because they are habitual, like whether someone will brush their teeth in the morning. You have a lovely smile. Chances are good that brushing is part of your daily routine."

"That's guessing, not foretelling."

"It's not guessing. I've seen every outcome."

"So why can't you just tell me what to do to get myself to the best conclusion?"

"Because telling you would change the final result. I can guide you, but ultimately, you are the one who has to make the decisions."

"I'm so confused."

"Here is something that you can bank on. I am here for you, Iris. I will guide you when you ask for it. I will celebrate with you when you are happy. I will hold you when you're sad. And I'll stay with you when you're scared. Your enemies are my enemies. Your family and friends are my family and friends. And when it comes time to fight, I will be at your side until the end."

"I'm not looking for a boyfriend or a husband. I can't do until death do we part with another person."

He let go of my hands and paced the small space from the sink to the sofa. "I'm not trying to be your boyfriend or your husband."

"Then what are you trying to be?"

"Whatever you need. It's not just my job. It's my life's purpose. You are the reason I exist."

His sincerity ramped up my anxiety, and my chest squeezed. What Keir offered was such a lopsided deal that it made my heart hurt for him. Blind devotion didn't leave a lot of room for free will. "I need my grass cut, my gutters cleaned, and my leaky faucet fixed. This..." I pointed between us. "...I don't need."

"I'm not trying to frighten you, Iris. You need my help to understand your abilities before the supermoon lunar eclipse. Give me these next couple of days to save your life."

"I'm not Arthur Pendragon. I'm a nobody from Southill Village." Only, I wasn't a nobody, was I? I was a witch—a witch with unpredictable powers. I held out my wrist to Keir and stripped the bandage. "This happened today when Evan was at the house."

The bark-like adhesion was the size of a quarter now.

Keir ran his finger lightly over the rough surface. He turned my arm and took the bandage from my forearm, then examined that one as well. "It was a protection spell," he finally said. "You wanted thicker skin so you wouldn't hurt."

"How do you know that?"

His smile was sad. "It's one of a thousand scenarios I've seen for you. I don't always remember them all, and there are aspects of your future that I just can't see. But what I have seen, I see with more precision once you've made a decision."

"That's both confusing and horrific. How can you function with all that going on in your head?"

"Do you have conversations in your head where you play out scenarios?"

"Yes. Quite a lot, actually."

"And you hear song lyrics? You think about a childhood memory. You worry about your son. Or any manner of things, like stuff on your to-do list."

"Speaking of to-do lists, I still have to get groceries today."

Keir's hand slipped into mine. I should have pulled away, but it just felt so damn good when he touched me. "So your brain is constantly going?"

"Sometimes it's on so much I can hardly sleep. So much noise."

His eyes softened as his lips curled up into a smile. "How do you manage to do your job? Keep your house? Raise your son? And any number of the other things you take care of daily with all that noise in your head."

"I'm used to it." I nodded, finally getting it. Damn. Linda was right. I could be a little slow. "You're used to it. It's just the noise in your brain."

Keir raised his brows. "Exactly."

"So," I said. "You want me to give you four days of trust until I get through this terrifying do-or-die magic test?"

"Yep." He gave me a crooked grin. "That's what I want."

"And after that?"

My question made him laugh. "Let's take it one crisis at a time."

I couldn't help but smile. "That's the story of my life, pal."

He smiled back. "I know."

# CHAPTER 13

"CAN I OFFER YOU SOMETHING TO DRINK?"

"What do you have?"

"I have beer and canned water."

"So many options," I smirked. "I still have to drive a half-hour back to town and shop for groceries, so I'll pass on the beer."

"Water then?" he asked.

Did I want to risk having to pee a second time before I got home? No, I did not. "Nah. I'm good. I have to go soon." I looked at the single sink run by a foot pump. "How do you keep the beer and water cold?"

"The beer is in a solar cooler, and I have a case of water in the closet."

"First, I should've guessed about the solar cooler, but where in the world do you have a closet in this place?"

"It's next to the toilet."

"I've peeked behind the curtain, future guy. There's no closet in there."

He grinned. “Follow me.”

I stood up. “Guide me, oh wise one.”

Keir’s handsome and slightly pretty face was awash with levity. “Your wish is my command.”

I chuckled until I remembered he’d said he’d been born bonded to me. “Not really, though, right? Like, you don’t have to do what I say, or anything like that, do you?”

His expression turned so serious it made me squirm. “Yes.”

I felt the blood drain from my face. “I…I…how can…I,” couldn’t formulate complete sentences. Probably a good thing. What if I accidentally told Keir to go to hell? Would he get a shovel and start digging? Ahh! This was too much responsibility.

Keir’s frown turned up at the corners, and he grinned. “I’m just messing with you, Iris. I promise you.” He placed his hands onto my shoulders. “I have complete free will.”

I smacked him in the chest. “You asshole.” When he didn’t react. I struck him again.

He grabbed my hand and held it over his heart. “I have made a commitment, Iris Everlee. This means I had a choice. I am my own man, ruled by none but myself.”

“But you said…”

“And I meant it. Every word.” His gray eyes swirled, and I swear I saw flecks of gold. “I have done all the preparations needed to help you, to guide you, to protect you, and to fight by your side. You are my calling, Iris. But, no, you are not the boss of me.”

I felt the tension ease around my eyes. “Okay,” I said softly.

He kept my hand as he tugged me toward the space

under the loft. He pulled back the curtain and put his fingers on a half-circle handle on the wall where the toilet paper roll hung. It slid forward, revealing three drawers, a clothes rod with several suits hanging on it, and under the drawers was a case of canned water.

"So much room. Is that your entire wardrobe?"

He chuckled. "I have hiding places all over this house."

"This isn't a house," I told him. "This is a shoebox with windows."

There was barely any room where we were standing, and Keir's hip brushed my stomach.

"Pardon me," he said politely, but he didn't move away.

I stared up at him. His dark eyelashes weren't thick, but they were longer than mine. Why was that always the way? His nose was narrow and aquiline, his cheekbones high. And gosh, he had a sensual mouth, wide but not so broad that it didn't fit his face. His upper lip was slightly fuller than his lower. In other words, super kissable. I hadn't been this close to a man for well over a year, and, according to doctors and psychologists, I was at my sexual peak.

Keir cleared his throat, and the intensity of his gaze made me nervously glance away. God, did he know I was thinking about kissing him? About sex? Ugh.

"We should, uhm, look at the grimoire before I go."

"Yes, absolutely," Keir agreed. He scooted past me quickly as if I were a hot poker, and he was trying not to get burned. "The book belonged to the first of your family. One of the witches of Islandmagee."

"You and Blondie said I was a descendant from that place. What is it? Who were these witches?" I sat back down on the couch, picked up the grimoire, and placed it on my lap. "Does this mean you know the woman who gave birth to me?" I wouldn't call her my mother. That title was strictly reserved for Grace Everlee.

"I'm afraid I don't. I vaguely remember your mother's face from my visions of your birth, but it's been forty-three years and a handful of days. And in my defense, I was only hours old. I've had millions of visions, along with living my life, since then."

"Did you ever have a vision of me meeting her? I mean, as an adult?"

He looked away for a moment then shook his head. "I'm sorry, Iris. She's either deceased or..."

"She really has no interest in being a part of my life." I shrugged. "I'm actually fine with that." I could feel the lie in my words. A couple days ago, I'd been content to never know where I came from before my parents took me in, but now, knowing I was a witch left me with so many questions for her. "So what do you know?"

"When I came into my moon, the circle I belong to was able to trace your tru-craft back to the Magee coven."

"What do you mean by you came into your moon? It sounds like a menstrual cycle for druids."

His eyes danced with humor. "There is bleeding, but it doesn't last long, and no sanitary pads are required."

I patted the book and got back to the Magees. "Are they still around? The coven, I mean."

He shook his head sadly. "Eight of the twelve were murdered between 1710 and 1711 during the witch trials."

"And what happened to the other four?"

Keir sat down next to me. "My guess is they found ways to hide in the mundane world, or they moved. There isn't much written about the witches. The one thing we do know is that Islandmagee has a history steeped in blood and tragedy."

"So, you don't know why the woman who squeezed me out of her hoo-ha gave me up when I was six months old?"

Keir shook his head. "I'm sorry, I don't."

I'd had a good life with my parents and my siblings, and I always tried to look at the fact that my birth mom had given me up as a blessing. My family was the best. But finding out I had a magical bloodline put my birth story into a whole different light. Had my mother known what I was? Had she been a witch? Or maybe it had been my father? After all, Linda said Michael would eventually develop powers, too.

"You should look to your grimoire," Keir said as if he could read my mind, which I sincerely hoped wasn't a thing. "They are the embodiment of your family's legacy."

I placed my palm over the symbol and felt it pulsing as if it were alive. I lifted my hand away. "I'm afraid to look. All this craziness started after this one bit me."

"Bit you?"

"One of the silver threads broke and poked the tip of my finger."

"Ah." He stared off for a moment as if in deep reflection before turning his gaze back to me. "I see it now. Your blood activated the magic contained within the pages."

"But the pages are blank. There is nothing on them." I fought back my frustration. "I'm not sure the book can give me the answers I want."

"It will give you the answers you need, Iris."

"Okay, Mick Jagger."

He chuckled. "Rolling Stones aside, the books are meant to unleash your tru-craft."

I'd been drawn to that box of books. And if the grimoire had belonged to my family, how had it ended up with Old Lady Boothwell? What if Keir had put it there himself to force my magical hand? The hairs on the back of my neck raised at the possibility. "How did you know the book would be at the auction? Did you put it there for me to find?"

"A witch's family grimoire has its own unique power. I have a feeling this book has been searching for you for a long time. I may have initiated the nudge to get you there, but if you hadn't gone to the estate sale, the grimoire would have found you another way." He gestured to the giant tome. "Open the book, and let's see if it's ready to reveal itself to you."

"You do it," I said, full of apprehension.

"Nope," he said, then gave me a tight-lipped smile. "See, I don't have to do something just because you say so."

"Yeah, but you could do it because it would be the nice bonded-buddy thing to do, right?"

"Not even then. This grimoire will only respond to you. When you blooded this one, it activated your terra-craft. Now, you have to get it under control."

I scratched the spot on my arm. "Right. Wild magic bad."

"Super bad."

I focused my resolve. "Should I get the crystal from my purse? Linda said to bring it along."

"It will help when it comes to learning spells, but we're not going to be doing any of that right now." He rubbed his hands together eagerly. "Let's just see what we're working with here."

His enthusiasm surprised me. "You're like a kid in a candy store."

"I didn't have to become a teacher of the occult. I did it because I actually dig this stuff. And, come on, a grimoire from the lost Magee coven. That's a serious find."

"Nerd," I teased. I traced the symbol. The upside-down triangle with the line through it. "You said at the auction that you knew what this symbol meant."

"It is the Earth element sign. It is the signal of the element you have the most affinity for."

"Oh." That made sense since Linda had been waiting in my garden for me to spark for several years. She must have known my magic would be tied to Earth stuff. "Okay. I'm going in." I flipped the cover open, careful this time to keep my fingers from getting pricked.

"That's strange," I said. "I think the inscription has changed."

*Blood of my blood, your sacrifice received.*

*Tears of my tears, do not be deceived.*

*Know yourself, child, lest your Magick be wild.*

*Now it's begun. It cannot be undone.*

*Goddess, help you.*

"What did it say before?"

"It had said that blood was the sacrifice required, and that the sacrifice would bring what I desired, and that I shouldn't enter into this lightly because once it was started, it couldn't be undone."

"Wow," Keir said with awe. "It's living text."

I gave him a bland look. “Have you never seen a grimoire before?”

“Several.” He moved his hand around over the page. “But none that were activated. This is amazing.”

“I’m so glad you’re excited. It sounds pretty awful for the poor soul who accidentally made a blood offering to the damn thing.”

“I’m sorry, Iris. Of course, you’re right.” But by the way he was eyeballing the book, I could see he still thought it was pretty damned cool. “Turn the page, let’s see what’s next?”

I did as he asked. Words began to appear—names without dates in different handwriting styles and different inks.

*Aideen Magee, 1678*

*Clionna Doon, 1705*

*Siobhan Adrian, 1782*

*Mary Ann Langford, 1834*

*Brigit O’Malley, 1880*

*Mira Roberts, 1912*

“Who are these women?”

Keir put his hand on my back and gave me a comforting pat. “These are your ancestors, Iris. The ones who have possessed the book in the past.”

“The last one was dated 1912. That’s too old to be my mother, right?” I mean, who knew? Maybe witches lived a long time.

“It would have been your grandmother, maybe a great grandmother.”

“So, no one had the book after Mira?”

He furrowed his brow as he made a study of the names. "It doesn't look like it."

"But none of them have the same last name."

"Traditionally, women took their husband's names. Or maybe some of them were adopted, like you."

Duh. Up until a couple weeks ago, I'd been Iris Callahan for eighteen years.

Keir went outside for a moment then came right back with his phone in his hand.

"I thought you didn't have any cell phone service up here?"

"I don't," he said. "I'd had to drive down the mountain about five miles to text you earlier. However, the camera feature does work. Can I take a picture of the names? I can do some research for you tomorrow and reach out to some of my contacts to dig up as much information on these women for you. But only if you want."

I touched the list of names, the vellum smooth under my fingertip. "Did you know what you were?" I asked them. "Or were you blindsided as well?" Clionna Doon would have been around during the Islandmagee witch trials. Had she escaped? Maybe. Or maybe, she'd been murdered, and her family, a daughter or a son, had escaped with the book. I wanted to know. "Yes, I want you to find out as much about them as you can."

Keir held up his phone. "May I?"

I moved my hand, so he had a clear shot of the list. He snapped the picture.

"Wait," he said. "There's more writing coming up."

*Claim your birthright, this book of shadows.*

*The Fade or The Bright, your intention hallows.*

*It starts with a name.*

*Goddess, help you.*

"Why does it always have to sound like a threat?" I asked.

"It seems the book wants your name."

"I got that." However, I wasn't ready to write it down. I'd given the book what it wanted the night before, and it had given me the stuff of nightmares. "I'm going to have to think about it."

"Don't take too long," Keir said. "The sooner you bind the book to you, the sooner you can learn the secrets of your tru-craft."

"That's what I'm afraid of." I inhaled deeply to bolster my strength. Magic, or tru-craft, was happening to me whether I liked it or not. It wasn't a pile of laundry or a sink full of dishes I could put off until later. The patches on my arm burned and ached as a reminder of just how much I couldn't ignore it. Besides, if I allowed this magic to kick my butt and turn me into dust, what would happen to Michael? And without me, would he fall to the same fate of not knowing who or what he was? Would he burn out as well? I wouldn't let that happen. I wouldn't abandon my child the way I'd been abandoned.

My gaze pivoted from the book to Keir. "Do you have a pen?"

# CHAPTER 14

THE NEXT DAY I AWOKE WITH BARK-SKIN CLEAR UP TO MY elbow. My arm itched like crazy. I sprayed it with Benadryl spray, covered it in cortisone, and even coated it in oil to see if it would soften up. No avail. If things kept going the way they were, I would soon look like Treebeard from the Lord of the Rings.

The only thing I could do was cover the eyesore until I could figure out how to deal with it. So, I cut a hole in a sock and used the tube to cover my gross-looking skin.

Neither Keir nor Linda had been helpful when it came to reversing the spell.

Michael had been up all night killing zombies and werewolves with his online pals, so the kid would be zonked until late in the afternoon. I didn't have to worry about him getting up and coming to the garden any time soon.

"I can't go on like this, Linda," I said as I sat down on the bench. I removed the sock and showed her my arm. "This stuff is growing fast."

She wrinkled her nose and made a face. "Chances are good you'll be magic dust before it reaches your neck."

"That's not helpful," I said. "How in the world did I manage to do this to myself?"

"If you hadn't cast a spell in your kitchen, I might've been able to narrow it down."

"First, I didn't cast a spell. Second, what about the kitchen makes it so bad?"

"I'm not going to fight with you about something as plain as your nose, *Kleinkind*."

I'd finally looked up the words. *Kleinkind* was basically her calling me a toddler, which I didn't love, but it was better than floppy tits. *Kleinkind* was a sorcerer, which I'd already guessed. And *Leibling* was darling. The fact that she'd called me *Leibling* a couple of times had softened me to the old grump.

Linda hopped up on the garden bench. "Do you cook a lot?"

"Yes," I said. "I have a teenager who likes to eat."

"And do you cook with a lot of spices and herbs, like cinnamon, cloves, rosemary, basil, thyme, marjoram, bay, and the such?"

"Yep. I have a mega spice rack." I loved all kinds of flavors.

"Then there's your answer. One of those herbs or spices acted as an agent for your spellwork. Until you figure out which one, there is no reversing the action. This is why you study terra-craft before evoking it."

"So I don't end up an Ent?"

"Ents are not real."

"Well, neither was talking gnomes until they were." I

flexed my arm. The tendons were getting tight between my wrist and my elbow. What if what was happing on the surface was also happening in my muscles? Eep! "What if I brought the spice rack out here? You can tell me what each one is used for, and when we get to the one that makes you grow a thick skin, we'll set things right."

"Or, your neighbors will sprout limbs from their asses."

I blanched. "Is that a possibility?"

Linda quirked her head to the side. She shoved her hand in her pocket and pulled out a pipe. She put it to her lips and gave it a puff. Smoke billowed from her lips.

"Did you have lit tobacco in your pocket?"

"I'm made of stone, *Kleinkind.* It's not like I'm going to catch on fire."

"But your clothes?"

"Are also made of stone." She shook her head, consternation written all over her face. "Just when I start to think you're not so ignorant, you remind me how wrong I am."

"And just when I start to think I could love you, you're as mean as shit to me."

She raised a hairy brow. "Your idea about the spice rack has merit. Bring it to me."

"I have a lot of spices," I said.

"Learning about the power of herbs and aromatics is a good lesson."

In other words, she didn't care. I walked backward to the kitchen with an eye on the gnome the whole time. I was tired of getting pelted by dirt clods.

"You're learning," she cackled.

Inside, I grabbed a sturdy tote from under the counter and started chucking everything from my rack into it. When

I was done, the bag weighed thirty pounds. I had a few essential oils I threw in for good measure, lavender, peppermint, and tea tree. It dawned on me I had some fresh herbs as well in the fridge. I only took out items that had been here before my shopping trip. Cilantro, parsley, mint, garlic, and...kale...was kale an herb? I wasn't sure, so I threw it in as well. Oh, and I had some pickled peppers. Dried peppers were a spice, so the jar made it in the bag.

Now it felt about fifty pounds as I lugged it out to the gnome.

"Did you pack the kitchen sink?" Linda asked.

"Har har." I carefully put the bag down. Most of the spices were in glass bottles, and I didn't want the pickled peppers to break and spill vinegar everywhere. "Anything that seemed like it would fit the bill of an herb or a spice is in there."

Linda reached in and pulled out the peppers first and frowned. "Peppers are great for sexual mojo spells, but pickled peppers are bound to sour a relationship."

"Good to know." I scratched my arm. "But not for protection spells."

"Nope." Linda pulled out the cilantro. "Another love spell ingredient." The kale was next. "This should be tossed immediately."

"Is it dangerous?" I asked.

"No," Linda replied. "It's just gross."

I rolled my eyes. "Next."

She grabbed the parsley. "Hmm. This could have contributed. Parsley is extensively used in purification rituals, but it also is good in strength spells. Didn't you say your ex- *Arschloch* was thrown from you?"

I nodded. "Yep." A hint of a smile played on my lips. "He hit his head on the fridge."

Linda chuckled. "It's going in the maybe pile."

Basil was next. "Love and protection. Also, money," Linda said. "I'll put it in the maybe pile."

I made a mental note of the money aspect. Michael's senior year would be expensive.

Linda must've read it in my face because she added, "Every spell cost something. Sometimes that price is small, sometimes it's not."

"Like growing bark on my skin?"

She nodded. "Exactly. I can't imagine your intention when you wished for a thick skin meant turning into a tree. But the combination of getting that man away from you and growing a thick skin had this unintended consequence. Your price to pay."

"Ah," she said as she retrieved another bottle. "Bay leaves. These are great for banishing evil and negative energy from your home."

"I better buy a case of it then. Does it work on grouchy gnomes?"

Linda ignored me. "It's also good for physical feats. Your son's an athlete. You should grind up a little bay leaf to throw into his food before games."

"I'll wait until I've mastered something easy...you know, like not destroying myself."

"Fair enough," Linda said. "Ah-ha, here's some oregano. Another one good for love and protection spells."

"There sure are a lot of these things used for love spells."

"Earth is the most romantic of all the elements."

"Yes, rocks and dirt are so sexy." I lifted my affected arm. "And my bark-shake brings all the boys to the yard."

"Dolt," she muttered. "Diamonds and gold are earth elements, too. Are you saying they're not sexy?"

She had me there. We spent the next two hours going over each herb and spice, with Linda spending several minutes on each one. She explained their properties, how they were activated with tru-craft, and how each one gave witches the ability to practice magic without paying a personal toll. The herbs and spices, and even the essential oils, paid the price instead.

Linda thinned her lips at me as she dug through the bag for the next item. Her face lit up as she pulled a small bottle out. "*Wunderbar*!"

"What did you find?"

"Peppermint oil." She snapped her fingers at me. "Go get your grimoire."

"But it's still empty, other than the incantation and the other witches' names."

"It won't be for long, *Kleinkind*. Do as I ask."

It had been more of an order than a request, but I didn't argue with her. "I'm going."

"And bring a pen," she said. "One that has special meaning for you, if you can manage. An heirloom, possibly."

I didn't have anything like that. However, I had the ballpoint Keir had given me the day before, and as far as special goes, well, I'd used it to seal myself to the grimoire. That was monumental, right? Speaking of Keir, I was waiting for him to message me about his research, so I checked my phone. I had one message, but it wasn't from the dashing druid professor. It was from a number I didn't recognize.

*Hey, Iris. This is Lu from the other night. I forgot to text so you'd have my number. Call me if you need a night out.*

That was so nice. It'd been a while since I'd hung out with anyone that wasn't my kid or a sibling. I didn't count Linda or Keir because their presence was directly related to me getting magical powers, not for fun.

I texted her back. *Busy every day for the next week. Work stuff. Let's have lunch the first week of June.* If I was still alive, that is. I didn't say that, though.

*It's a date, but only if you make it drinks and dancing*, she messaged back.

I giggled. *You got it.*

It was oddly comforting having one aspect of my life that didn't revolve around my divorce, my kid, or tru-craft.

Bob jumped up on my table and meowed at me.

I gave him the stink eye. "If Linda sent you in here to hurry me up, I'm hurrying," I told him.

He made cutesy squeaks that I swear sounded like denials.

"I'm just teasing you, Bob. I know you wouldn't do me like that." I wore my favorite yoga pants today, aka they had pockets, so I tucked the phone in them. Dear designers, I thought ruefully, pockets belong in all of women's wear.

I retrieved the grimoire from my bedroom, peeked in on Michael—still snoring away—and hustled back out to the garden.

I set it on the bench and opened it up. "Now what?"

Linda rubbed her stubby fingers together. "This is a milestone, *Leibling.*"

"What is?"

"The recording of a first spell." She gestured to a paving stone in front of the bench. "Sit."

I did, but I swore if she told me to "stay" I was going to knock her gnome block off.

Bob wormed his way under my arm and curled in my lap. "What a sweet little chonky-chonk," I cooed.

The imp-cat body vibrated pleasantly as he purred.

"Good," Linda said. "The imp will help you focus the spell."

I scratched under Bob's chin. "I thought you said I wasn't ready for spells."

"We're not doing it yet." If Linda had been carrying a ruler, she'd have smacked me with it. "You must understand a spell and how it works before you invoke it. That's how you control the tru-craft instead of casting with your emotions."

"What do I do first?"

"This is a rudimentary spell. You will have to add a variation to make it yours. This is why it's so important to understand the materials you work with."

"I guess peppermint is part of it."

"Yes," Linda said. "Not only does it smell great and keep mice away, but it is also a clarifying agent. Your magic knows what ingredients it drew from to cast the spell. I can't help you undo the work, but I do know how to create a clarifying and seeking potion. If you can get it right, it should show you how the spell was crafted."

"So, this is a potion?"

"Yes. I don't possess tru-craft, but you don't have to be a practitioner to understand and utilize nature." She steepled her fingers. "Do you have your pen?"

"Yep." I pulled the ballpoint from my pocket. "Got it right here." I opened the book to the first empty page. "Ready."

"Five drops of peppermint oil, a teaspoon of ground bay leaf, grind threc leaves of basil, add a pinch of cinnamon, and a pinch of sage."

"My sized pinch or yours?" I asked as I scribbled it all down.

"Yours," Linda said, giving me an approving look. "Do you have any chamomile in the house?"

"Yep. I have some chamomile tea that has been sitting around since before my mother died. She was the only one who could drink the stuff. Does it matter how old it is?"

"It should be fine," Linda said. However, I didn't love her worried expression. Note to self: buy chamomile that hasn't expired.

"What else?"

"It's your turn to make the potion your own." Linda dumped the bag out onto the grass. "Are there any of these ingredients that are calling to you?"

My skin had been buzzing since I'd signed the book. It was hard to feel anything else. Then I spotted the anise. I used the licorice tasting spice occasionally when I made Chinese food. However, it wasn't the taste that attracted my attention. It was the shape. The anise, also called star anise, reminded me of the scar on Keir's wrist. I picked up the bottle. "This one," I said.

Linda nodded. "Add two to the mix."

"What do I mix it with?"

"You'll want purified water."

"Will distilled water work?" I kept a jug for my mini steam cleaner.

"That'll do. One cup of the water, bring it to a boil in a glass pot. Add the spell ingredients, stir with a non-metal spoon, and let it steep for fifteen minutes."

I had a glass measuring cup I could heat the water in. "Does it matter if I microwave the water?"

Linda shook her head. "No, that'll do."

"Then what?"

"Then you draw yourself a bath, dump the potion in."

"Strain or no strain?"

"No strain."

"Yuck, but okay." I didn't relish the idea of little bits of herbs getting caught in my cracks, but I'd do what needed to be done. "Anything else?"

"Repeat your intention for the potion taking deep breaths in between until the potion works."

I nodded then wrote down the rest of the directions down. "What should I say?"

"Do I have to do everything for you, *Kleinkind*? Words. You tell the potion what you want, and you focus on your intention. The potion will help set the limit. Do not let your thoughts stray. Ask for the clarification you need. Ask for guidance. Then relax and let the magic function as it should."

"Is this a good idea?"

"Potion spells aren't as dangerous. You are borrowing energy from the ingredients, not yourself. You will be fine. Take the imp with you. He can help you focus your limits." As she walked back to her spot in front of the bench, she muttered, "I hope."

"I heard you, Linda." Great. I was going to try a spell again. What could possibly go wrong? "If I boil my ass, you're going to feel really bad."

"I'd be more worried about turning to dust. Boiling your ass is a step up. Go. Do." She flicked her hand at me then turned back to stone.

## CHAPTER 15

THANKS TO LINDA'S GAME OF 52-SPICE JAR PICK-UP, I HAD to spend several minutes gathering up all the kitchen items to bring back into the house. The gnome ignored my muttered curses.

What were the odds that I could steep my potion and get into the bath before Michael got up? Did it matter? He'd seen me through several diet fads, including this past month of kale. Kale shakes, kale chips, stir fry kale, kale salads, and so on. The leafy green veg wasn't too bad as long as you liked eating dirt. I hadn't, which was why I had a whole bag left over.

Linda had been right. Kale *is* gross.

I threw the bag away before putting the other items, except for the ingredients I needed, away.

I kept the distilled water in the laundry room. I dusted the top of the jug and realized it had been a long time since I'd used the steam cleaner. I grimaced. I hoped distilled water didn't expire.

*Nah,* I thought. *It's fine.*

I was hesitant with the chamomile, but it was packaged in a foil pouch, so it still smelled like it would make tea. I boiled the water in my four-cup Pyrex measuring cup, then mixed in the ingredients with a wooden spoon as Linda had directed. My energy hummed pleasantly inside me as I stirred counterclockwise. I guessed my magic was happy with what I was doing. That made one of us.

I set the timer for it to steep when Michael came sauntering into the kitchen. "Morning." His eyes were swollen in an *I've been up all night staring at a giant television screen without blinking* kind of way.

"Morning, babe. Are you up for the day, or are you going back to bed?" It was only ten a.m., and I'd fully expected he wouldn't be getting up until much later.

"I told Doug I'd come over and shoot some hoops this morning." He rubbed his eyes, and I could see he clearly regretted his decision.

"You can always cancel or tell him you'll come over later. I bet he isn't even out of bed."

Michael sighed and pulled his phone out of his shorts' pocket because, of course, men had pockets in everything. "He's blowing up my text." He showed me his screen with a dozen messages from Doug telling Michael to get up, get up, get up.

My phone beeped. I slipped it from my pocket to sneak a peek, hoping it was Keir. It was not.

*Is Michael awake?*

I showed my son my screen. "Doug is very persistent." I snapped a picture of the kid flipping off the phone and sent it to Doug with a *He's up*.

Doug sent back several thumbs-up emojis.

"Will you be gone long?" Having him out of the house when I worked my mojo in the tub was to my advantage. At least if I blew up the bathroom, he wouldn't be here to see it.

Note to self: ask Linda to cover my body if the spell kills me, so my son doesn't have to see his dead mamma naked.

I wasn't really worried about dying. If Linda was confident, then so was I. Anyway, I was more likely to turn to dust than leave a corpse behind.

"I'm going to stay the night if that's okay."

"Sure." I narrowed my gaze on him. "If there's any drinking or drugging, there will be no driving, and if you get into trouble, you call me right away."

"Yep," he said, blinking his eyes until he could get them wider than slits. "Did you wash my gray joggers?"

I hadn't washed clothes in a week. Thankfully, I had ten gazillion pairs of stretchy yoga pants and loose flowing tops. Most importantly, I had enough underwear to last me several months without running out of clean pairs. I exaggerate, of course, but only a little. "You know where the laundry soap is."

He frowned and said, "Why does it stink in here?" as he left the kitchen.

"Love you too," I yelled after him. *Good,* I thought, *kid out. Operation clarification is a go.*

I heard the washing machine start up and smiled. *Eggggg-cellent.* My evil plan to turn him into an independent adult was working.

Another beep of my phone had me cursing. "Damn it, Michael. Text Doug back!"

"I did!" he yelled back.

I opened my messages. "Oh." It was Keir, finally.

*Found some history on 3 of your ancestors. Is now a good time to come over?*

*Give me an hour.* I wanted to try the clarification spell before Keir arrived. Hopefully, Michael would be on his way to Doug's by then. Or, even better. *If I don't answer the door, please come in and hide the body.*

*What???*

I shot him back a thumbs up like Doug had with me. If the man who could see thousands of my futures playing out and exploding in a tub wasn't one of them, then yay me.

The timer went off on the potion. I should have been scared. All this freaking stuff happening to me was flippin' scary. Instead, I was excited.

I grabbed the measuring cup. "Ouch. Still hot." I adjusted my grip on the handle. I exited the kitchen and headed to my private bathroom in the master bedroom. I heard the second bathroom shower turn on.

"Don't use all the hot water!" I yelled to Michael. His music started playing loudly, so I couldn't be sure if he heard me. I set the potion down on the vanity. When Evan and I picked this place, we'd both loved the *ensuite* bathroom. It had a large walk-in shower for him and a separate garden tub for me. Now, both the shower and the tub were all mine. Michael's bathroom was just on the other side of the wall. I wasn't sure I would find my Zen to do the clarification spell with Gypsy Punk blaring in the background. Although it was better than the K-pop, but not by much.

Actually, I didn't mind any of the music most of the time, but I needed some peace and quiet right now.

I wanted to center myself, so I left the smelly herbal minty potion in the bathroom and went back outside to the garden.

"Did you do it?" Linda asked.

"Not yet." I sat on the bench. "Waiting for the kid to leave." I glanced at the gnome, who wasn't moving anything but her lips at the moment. "Does it matter if the stuff cools down?"

"Nope," she said. "Most witches bottle the potions and sell them."

"So, I can make this a side hustle if I need a little cash, huh?" I grunted. "Good to know."

"If you can stay alive long enough."

"I'm really getting tired of your Debbie-downer attitude, Linda."

"And I'm just really tired, *Leibling*."

I stared at the gnome. Was she paler than usual? And why wasn't she animating? "Is something wrong?"

"I just need to rest," she said. "Moving above ground is difficult for my kind. We are not creatures of the air. It takes effort."

"You always seem to move so fast."

"It's my age. I'm still a youngling, and that comes with agility. Even so."

"You're two hundred years old."

"Yes. Not that long ago, I was a twinkle in my daddy's eye." She paused for a moment. "I didn't want you to see me like this. I thought I'd have time to recharge, but I forget how needy young witches can be."

"Especially toddlers, like me, huh?"

I was being sarcastic. It was wasted on Linda. "Most especially," she lamented.

"Okaaaay. Good talk." I braced myself to get up then noticed pretty pink clusters of flowers on my cleome plant. Hmm. That didn't usually bloom until mid to late June.

I looked around the garden and saw that several of my flowers and flowering bushes were blooming.

"Linda, what's going on with the plants?"

She smiled. "They are called by your Earth magic. It's a good thing."

My eyes misted. The green leaves were greener, all the plants looked healthy and lush, and the flowers were all the colors of the rainbow. "My mom would have loved this," I whispered.

"Grace was a special woman," Linda agreed. "She had a connection to nature that cannot be taught." She shifted her eyes toward me and gave me a dull look. "No matter how much I wish it were so."

"We don't have to talk," I replied with the same lack of enthusiasm. "You rest up."

After about ten minutes of meditating on not scratching my arm off, I heard Michael yell from the kitchen window. "See ya."

A few seconds later, I heard his car start.

"Calgon, or in this case, clarification spell, take me away," I said.

"Finally, some alone time," Linda bitched.

Bob pounced on her head.

I laughed harder than I should have.

Linda expended effort she claimed she didn't have and shooed Bob away.

"Come on, my little chonky monster," I told him. "Let's leave the crotchety old gnome alone."

I let the water fill up in the tub as I undressed, tied my hair up in my bath turban, and poured the potion on in. Ick. It turned the water a greenish-gray, and the bits and pieces of herbs floated around. I climbed in and sat down.

"Cripes!" Something pinched my butt. I leaned to the side, and a single star anise floated to the surface. "This gig should come with hazard pay," I said as I flicked it away.

*Zen*, I thought. *Find the Zen.*

I took a deep breath and blew it out. "Let the hot water soak my cares away. Give me the strength to me this day. Guide me through the light and the dark. Help me get rid of this awful bark." Mentally, I added, *I want my damn skin back to normal. I didn't want actual thick skin. You're supposed to know my heart, according to Linda. So, now would be a good time for you to give me an accurate reading.*

In other words, I tried to keep my intention super transparent.

I took another deep breath and exhaled. "Help me see what I cannot see. An eye for the truth, you..." Shoot, these rhymes were not easy. I already had mad respect for poets, but now, it was doubly so. I exhaled again. "An eye for truth..." No, maybe mentioning my eye was a bad thing. I didn't want my misfiring magic to hit another body part. "A mind for the truth..." Better, I thought. "A heart not denied. This spell better work because I have clarified."

Once again, I sent it my intention. *And by clarified, I'm not talking about butter. I mean, I want to know what I need to know to survive all this intact and not covered in tree bark or any other organic or non-organic matter.*

This was starting to feel very much like bargaining with a Djinn. You had to be very specific because genies liked to loosely interpret your wishes. At least in fiction. I wasn't sure if real genies existed, and really, I wasn't sure I wanted to know. I had enough on my plate as it was.

I inhaled a few more times deeply as I let the minty scent wash over me.

The bathroom began to shake as the water around me sloshed. Bob, who'd been curled up on the toilet, rose up on his tippy-toes and hissed. A glass container with Q-tips jostled across the vanity and smashed on the floor.

"What is going on?" Surely, this wasn't a side effect from me splitting the pool the day before. I pulled the plug on the drain and carefully got out of the tub so I wouldn't cut my feet on the broken glass.

The quaking subsided, but a loud *Pop!* had me racing to throw my clothes on.

One leg in my pants and one leg out, I hopped through the house. When I got to the kitchen, I looked out the window and gasped. Linda was fighting a ten-foot rock with arms and legs, and there was a massive hole in the center of my garden.

I grabbed a knife from the knife drawer. Would a knife work on a rock? I threw it in the sink and grabbed a hammer from the utility drawer. Better.

I raced outside to help my gnome, with Bob hot on my heels.

"I swear this wasn't me," I told Linda.

"I know, *Kleinkind*," she said. "This is one of the rock trolls I warned you about. And it is starving for your magic."

## CHAPTER 16

I HELD THE HAMMER ALOFT OVER MY HEAD, FEELING ridiculous. Grabbing the ball-peen was like bringing a knife to a gunfight. The gun, in this case, was a stupidly large rock beast covered in vines and hanging moss and could crush me with its pinky toe.

"How do we stop this thing?"

Linda, who looked as freaked out as I felt, shook her head. "I've already tried to sing him home, but he won't budge. The *bertroll* is determined to have you."

"Well, he can't," I snapped. I shook my hammer at the troll. "You can't have me."

His response was to send down a crashing fist toward my head.

I jumped out of the way, but he nearly nailed me! I was already breathing hard when I rolled to my feet. Linda's game of dirt dodging had not adequately prepared me from Whack-a-Troll. If I got out of this alive, I promised myself I would start working out with Rose.

"Tell me what to do," I begged Linda.

"Run!" she shouted. "Keep it busy. Contain it within the gates. A troll on the loose in town will be hard to explain."

"You think?" Oh my, word. I hadn't run in years. However, when the troll took a giant step in my direction, the adrenaline rush was the wind beneath my wings. I dashed to the back of the yard. The stupid troll crushed a bunch of my plants when it followed after me. I went back and forth between keeping the troll in the backyard or leading it through the gate. I would survive the people of Southill Village finding out that there were more than just humans living in our neck of the woods. I couldn't claim the same odds of surviving the rock monster trying to eat me if I stayed put.

"Num, num," the troll said. "Get in my tum."

Eep! It talked. In actual words. I was officially freaking out.

He swiped a massive paw at me, his fingertips brushing my head and sending me careening face-first into the fence. I smashed my nose and let out an angry cry.

I whipped around. "No!" I screamed. "Stop!"

Surprisingly, the grotesque beast did as I asked.

"Mortle want." He opened and closed his hammy fist, indicating he wanted me to walk to him.

"No, thank you."

His thick, bushy brows knitted together as his lips curled into a snarl. "Mortle want magic."

Was his name Mortle? I was guessing so. "Mortle can suck a big, slimy toad."

He looked back and forth on the ground. "Where toad?"

His skin had a gray cast to it that reminded me of the

bark on my arm. He was moving closer to me. What in the world was Linda doing? Why was I handling this by myself? My feet felt frozen to the ground as the weight of what was happening settled in.

"Linda!"

"Figure it out," she said. "I'm busy."

Busy doing what? It certainly wasn't saving me. Some Earth guardian she was turning out to be.

I needed to think. To formulate a plan. What was a rock troll's weakness? Other than fictional stories of trolls under bridges who hid treasures and ate babies, I had little knowledge about the terrible creatures. The fear that kept me frozen in place eased and as an eerie calmness settled over me.

When I was in the tub asking for clarity, this was the exact situation where it would've come in handy.

The nards! Linda called the troll a *he*, and males typically had testicles. Even my butthole-free imp had them. If I could get close enough without getting pummeled, I could probably nail him with the hammer in his happy place. At my core, I knew my plan was awful, but I had nothing else.

As if Bob knew I was thinking about him, he leaped onto the troll's head gouged at his eyes with his claws. My hope soared. Bob was the distraction I needed.

I ran up to the troll, coming in low while he swung his arms, windmill-style, trying to dislodge the imp. I slid like a baseball player between the troll's legs and swung the ball peen with all my might.

The terrifying rock beast didn't even flinch. Instead, it flung Bob from his head, and reached out a surprisingly fast hand, and grabbed me around the waist.

"Linda," I gasped out. "A little help."

The ground beneath me gave out. I screamed as I fell twenty feet down with the rock troll next to me. When we landed, I was thrown a good five feet from him, but the walls were steep and built with smooth, red and gray igneous rock. In other words, I was trapped!

"*Leibling!*" Linda shouted. "I built the trap for the troll, not you. What are you doing down there?"

"Dying, obviously," I told her. "Christ, Linda. Get me out of here."

Bob jumped down into the pit. The troll smashed him under his foot.

"No!" I screamed. "Leave him alone."

Mortle began to laugh. Or, at least, I thought he was laughing as he twisted his foot over my precious Bob and ground him into the ground.

"I'll kill you," I screamed, launching myself at the troll. My attack surprised Mortle because he staggered back.

Bob wasn't moving and his body looked like some had driven a steamroller over it. I yanked on of the vines growing out of the troll's neck with one hand and punched him in the face with the other. The troll grabbed my hand and chomped down on my arm—the one with the bark. The pressure was painful, but it didn't break the skin. With my non-barky hand, I jammed my thumb into the rock trolls watery globe of an eye.

It roared as it tried again to bite through my arm. The thick skin didn't even crack.

It was risky, but what did I have to lose. He'd killed my Bob, and since my entire body wasn't covered in the impervious bark, soon, he would kill me, too. I could do this. I fractured an entire community pool with my thoughts. How hard could a rock troll be?

I stared at Mortle in his one good eye. "I'm going to pop your head like a melon," I promised. "Crack, crack," I said. "Down the middle, you will split. Crack, crack, you gigantic piece of shit." I filled my words and my magic with so much intention, I worried that I would indeed break the mountain as the sound of lightning echoed through the four walls of the cage Linda had built. I don't know who looked more surprised, Mortle or me, as he divided in two, both halves of him, flopping to the ground, and me along with him.

I learned a couple things about rock trolls at that moment. One, they are not solid rock like you might think. Nope. They are full of blood and guts and even a tiny amount of brain. And two, their insides stink worse than their outsides.

Linda tunneled out the base. "This way!" she shouted. Her face blanched when she saw me lying in the troll goo. "What happened?"

A gasping sob escaped me. "He...he...he...Bob. He killed Bob." Tears rolled down my cheeks, and I made the mistake of wiping at them with my gut-covered hands. I pointed at my flattened cat. "Oh, Bob."

Then the strangest thing I'd ever seen, and after the past couple of days, I'd seen a lot of weird shit, happened. Bob's smooshed body began to inflate. His paws, his head, his body, and his tail. There were cracks and hisses and squishy sounds that made my teeth ache. But in a matter of seconds, Bob was on his feet. He bounded over to me and jumped into my lap. He tipped his head up and licked me.

"Eww, Bob. Don't do that. I got gross troll yuck on me." I

didn't realize I was laughing until Linda started laughing too. What a ridiculous mess we were.

"I'm sorry I didn't get here sooner, Leibling. I had to make the tunnel big enough for you to get out," she said.

"It all worked out." I smiled fondly at Bob. "Didn't it, my goodest boy?" Bob purred in response. I held up my barky arm. "And believe it or not, this damn thing saved my life. Maybe the magic knew what I needed after all. Though, I really don't want to keep it."

"How did you do it?" Linda ask. "How did you defeat the rock troll?"

"I used your first lesson, and I cracked him like an egg."

She laughed. "I guess we're lucky the mountain is still standing."

"It was a concern," I admitted. "So you have a way out?"

Linda took off her hat, and underneath, her head was a shiny, hairless dome. "I've made a tunnel with stairs for you."

"You're bald," I said.

"Of course, I am, dolt." She yanked her hat back down to her ears. "Now get out of here, so I can start filling in the ground. It won't do for Michael or one of your many siblings to see any of this."

I stood up, but I was barefoot, and my feet were slick. I slipped in the ick, splashing down on my rear.

Linda snickered.

"Not funny," I said.

She shrugged. "We take our small pleasures where we can."

Bob made an almost howling sound. I think the smell was getting to him. I know it was getting to me.

"Iris?" a man said.

I looked up and saw Keir standing at the edge of the pit. "Are you okay?"

"Awesome timing," I said. "Keep this up, and I'm going to start calling you the Late Kreskin."

# CHAPTER 17

I SENT OUT A PRAYER OF THANKS TO WHOEVER WAS listening that Michael had gone to stay the night at Doug's house. Linda had called in the gnome donsy, and there were twelve near replicas of my grumpy guardian hard at work putting my yard back together.

There was a reason they were called garden gnomes. I'd showered Mortle off of me using an entire tube of body wash and half a bottle of shampoo in the process. Even when I looked clean, I could still smell him.

"I might need to buy some tomato juice," I said to Keir as I walked into the kitchen, drying my hair. "I think the troll was part skunk. I can still smell it."

Keir made a face. "It's bad. You might try hydrogen peroxide, baking soda, and the blue liquid dish soap. Some chemist discovered it neutralized skunk smells." He turned his head away as I crossed to the sink to look out the window. "You might want to air dry your clothes after you wash them because the dryer heat might bake the smell in."

"The only place those clothes are going is in a burn pile," I told him. Linda and her crew had already filled in the hole and were starting on sewing sod. "They are speedy." I was definitely impressed.

"Gnomes are of the Earth. It makes them efficient."

"And then some." My yard didn't look like a giant troll just tried to eat me anymore, so I was calling it a win. The fight had taken it out of me. At over forty, I didn't bounce back the way I used to. "I'm so tired," I said. "I don't know if I have the energy to fight anyone or anything else." The worry about what was coming next knotted my gut. "Do you think more will come?" Linda had mentioned fairies, elves, and trolls, along with the extremely dangerous *die Hexenmeister*. "I got lucky with the troll. I'm not sure I will get lucky anymore."

"I'm sorry I wasn't here. I was on my way into town before I knew what was happening. I saw so many..." He sighed. "I'm just grateful you made it."

"Me too." I braced myself against the counter. "I reacted with instinct today, Keir. I wasn't thinking about the costs. Now I'm scared. I took a life. Even if it was a gross troll that was trying to kill me. I would think something like that is going to exact a major price."

Keir nodded. "The price was paid by the rock troll. His death was the magic's price. Did Linda teach you about how ingredients work in a potion or a spell?"

I nodded.

"Those ingredients pay the cost of the magic. In this case, the troll was your ingredient."

I made a face. "How awful." I thought about what Linda had said about the *Hexenmeister*, how they sacrificed witches for the magic. Is that what I'd done? Had I sacrificed the troll, not to gain magic, but to satisfy it. Is that the way trucraft operated?

The overwhelming feeling of despair shook me. "How am I any different from the people who want to kill me to take my powers? Especially if I know that to use my magic, something has to die."

Keir braved my stench to stand beside me. He put his arm around me, and I leaned into his shoulder. "That's not always the case," he said. "Sometimes the price is happiness, joy...love."

"I don't understand."

"When you see Michael smile or laugh, how does it make you feel?"

I looked up at him. "Wonderful."

Keir smiled at me. "That's magic too."

"Thanks." I felt a little better, but I wasn't sure I completely believed him. When I'd been asked to pick between the Bright and the Fade, I hadn't been able to decide. And after I created the spell, I knew in my heart what it meant to be Bright. But killing the troll, it had been one hundred percent Fade. "Is my indecision about which path I should follow putting me in more jeopardy? Do you think that's why I'm more at risk of burning up?"

"I'm not going to lie to you, Iris. Knowing your path might help you get control of your magic. But the real risk is in your power. My order hasn't felt anything like your strength in a long time. It's both exciting and frightening."

"I thought you guys were all about finding witches and bonding with them."

He chuckled and shook his head. "What happened to me

when I was born is a rarity now, even as it was back in Merlin's day. Druids do seek out those of the tru-craft and act as guides. We seek to get as many to the other side of their magic without dying. It's one of our many acts of faith. But what I have with you, the way we are connected only happens once every millennium. You are the Arthur of this time."

"I will not be pulling a sword from a stone."

"Probably not," Keir smirked.

"And I won't be anyone's king. I can barely rule myself."

"You are so much more than you can even imagine, Iris."

"I have a pretty good imagination. Why don't you try me?"

He looked away. "I wish I could tell you."

"But telling me changes the future," I said.

Keir nodded. "What I can say is that what's coming will require you to be at your full strength, so you have to do everything possible to conquer terra-craft. It is the only way to protect yourself."

"I'll do whatever I have to do. I swear it." Especially if it meant keeping Michael and my family safe. "What did you learn about the women who signed the grimoire?"

"Not much about Aideen Magee or Clionna Doon. Those two would have originated at Islandmagee just north of Belfast in Ireland. But Siobhan Adrian lived down south on the coast in Galway until she died in 1784."

I sucked in a breath. "That's only two years after she signed the book."

Keir's brow furrowed. "It's true. She had two children. A son and a daughter. The daughter died at the age of sixteen, but the son survived."

"His name isn't in the book." I gave Keir a sharp look. "There are no men in the book."

He nodded. "That's true. Male witches often go their whole lives without a sparking event. Sometimes the women don't spark either. That's why it can seem as if whole generations pass before one of them becomes a practitioner of the true craft."

"But Linda said Michael was a witch. Does this mean he won't have any magic?"

"Michael is your son, so, yes, he is a witch. He'll always have the potential to spark, but it doesn't mean he will."

"What are his odds of a normal life?"

"With you for a mother?" He smiled. "Chances are good he'll be extraordinary. But the odds of him sparking are low. It always is for the men of your species."

"Would his element be Earth, like mine? Or something else?"

"Female witches are more prone to Earth and Water, while males are more likely to be Fire or Wind practitioners. The covens of old liked to have a nice mix of all five elements."

"Five?" What was left?

Keir took a piece of paper from the grocery list tablet hanging on the fridge. Next, he retrieved a pencil from my utility drawer, reminding me that my hammer was at the bottom of the pit with troll goop. He drew a pentagram with the star upright, and he finished it off with a circle around it. Each point of the star was giving a letter, S, W, F, E A, moving from the topmost point to the right in clockwise order. He pointed to the E.

"That's Earth," he said. "Terra-craft draw their power

from nature and Earth elementals like Linda the gnome." He went to A next. "Air. Aero-craft. Power comes from wind, of course, and it has its own elemental creatures like sprites and winged fae. The F is Fire. Igni-craft. The W is for Wind. Eurus-craft." He glanced at me then pointed to the top letter. "S," he said, "Is Spirit. Anima-craft. Its power is drawn from the very soul of the world. There are no elementals for this discipline. The magic involves channeling and summoning spirits to fuel spellwork. It's the most dangerous of the five. Anima-craft witches are rare because it is the most volatile of all the elements, and ninety-nine percent of the time, a novice witch will not survive to master it."

I shivered. The idea of dealing with ghosts and other spooky stuff, along with the increased likelihood of dying, made me glad I got something as mundane as Earth, trolls, and the like be damned. "I'm glad I got Earth now."

"And the fact that you've taken out a mountain rock troll will deter those who aren't serious about wanting to take your power from you."

"Yay me," I said without enthusiasm. There was something childlike about Mortle that, if he hadn't stomped my imp into the ground, I might have felt sorry for him. As if conjured, Bob weaved between my legs. I moved out from under Keir's arm and picked him up.

"You know he's modeled himself after a Manx cat. It is an Irish cat with a bobbed tail." He took his phone out of his pocket and searched for images in the browser. "Here, see?"

I bounced Bob in my arms as I looked at all his multi-colored and patterned twins. "They are adorable." I scratched Bob under the chin. "Just like you are."

Keir shook his head and chuckled.

"What?"

"That imp has you wrapped around his tiny claws."

"Damn right, he does."

"You know they're designed that way."

Linda had said something similar. That he was made for me to love. Or something to that effect. "What do you mean?"

"He's your familiar. You're spark pulled him from his realm and landed him on your doorstep. His biology is such that he emits hormones mixed with some impish magic to increase a witch's oxytocin level."

"The cuddle hormone?" I said with a laugh. I'd learned all about it when my Braxton-Hicks coach explained to us mothers and fathers how oxytocin was the hormone that made us fall in love with our babies. It was also true of puppies and kittens. Increased production made you literally want to cuddle with the object of your affection. Hence, the cuddle hormone. Increased oxytocin also made you feel good. And who couldn't use a little bit of that kind of magic? I gave Bob a gentle hug. "I don't care how the sausage is made. I'm happy to be eating it."

Bob yawned, his mouth stretched wide and his tongue out and curled.

I glanced at Keir. "How can you not love this face?"

"Because he's not trying to make me love him."

I shrugged. "Fair enough." I set Bob back on the floor. "You said you found out some stuff on three of the women. Who else?"

"Brigit O'Malley lived in York, England. She had to be a descendant of Siobhan Adrian's son. Still, I can't find much out about her family because she was a foundling and was put into an apprenticeship at a textile plant when she was around eight years old. When she was fifteen, she married a shoemaker named Roger O'Malley. She died in 1894 at the age of thirty-six during childbirth. It was her tenth pregnancy. Only two of her children survived beyond a few months."

The tragedy of all her losses broke my heart. "Who else?"

"Mira Roberts. The last to sign the book. She came over to the United States as a refugee during the first world war in 1914. I was able to find her immigration card, and it had her listed as being from France. She had one child listed, but the name was impossible to read. The husband was listed as deceased."

"So, she'd signed the book before coming to America."

He nodded. "And she probably remarried after she arrived in New York. Unfortunately, I couldn't find any sign of her except for the card. I search some French databases, but their records weren't much better."

"At least it's something," I said. "Do you think she brought the book? I can't imagine she would've been allowed to bring too many items with her."

Keir put his hand on mine. "It would have been hard for her to leave it behind. But maybe. Either way, the book made its way here, to this remote mountain village, to find you."

The gnomes were replanting the uprooted shrubs in the garden, and it was nearly back to its original beauty. "And with it," I said, "gnomes and trolls. And heaven only knows what else."

# CHAPTER 18

THE NEXT DAY, I AWOKE WITH EVERY SINGLE ONE OF MY muscles aching and on fire. Keir had stayed with me until the gnomes had finished their work, but I'd just been so tired and worn out, that I'd told him to go so I could get some sleep. He'd been reluctant, but I'd insisted. And now, after a good twelve hours of sleep, I hurt in places I didn't even know I could hurt. I groaned as I rolled sideways on my bed, my arms refusing to have any part of the process. Fighting a troll had taken its toll on me. So I lay there for a long moment contemplating whether to keep trying or just pee the bed.

I'd paid a lot of money for the mattress shortly after Evan had moved out. I didn't want to sleep in our bed, not with the Evan-sized dent on what had been his side. Nope. So, I dragged the mattress, by myself, out to the street curb the next day. My dad brought his truck over that afternoon and hauled it away for me. After, he took me shopping for a new one. I'd spent half the money in my savings account on a top-of-the-line foam mattress, guaranteed not to lose its shape for twenty years. It was the mattress I'd wanted years earlier, but Evan had said it was a luxury we couldn't afford since my work was so unstable.

Evan could bite me. My new bed was like sleeping on a hug, and I didn't regret one damn dime. And there was one other feature about the bed that I loved. I reached over to the nightstand, grabbed the remote control that I never used, and held down the top button. The head of the bed slowly began to rise. When it was all the way up, I managed to stand. I felt almost as victorious as I had when I'd defeated the troll. Until I started walking. Oh, damn, I would never ever snicker at my dad when he complained of achy joints. If he hurt even a fraction of what I did, the man deserved a medal for getting out of bed every morning.

I'd been so distracted by the pain that I hadn't noticed my barky arm was no longer covered in the gray, husky material. The tub potion must've worked. I let out a squee of joy, then dialed it back as I peed a little. Note to self: No celebrating until the bladder is empty.

With a lot of effort and a fair amount of cussing, I managed my morning routine of showering, brushing my teeth, sort of combing my hair—it was impossible to get my arms over my head—before dressing myself and starting the coffee pot. Bob followed me the whole time, vocally cheering me on with a lot of chirps and trills. When I got settled in with my first cup of java, I took two Tylenol and two ibuprofens and waited for the pain relievers to blissfully kick in.

Unfortunately, my doorbell rang before that happened. I wasn't expecting guests, and after the last few days, I wasn't looking forward to any more surprises.

I pulled the curtain back and peeked out the living room window to determine if I would treat my caller like a meat salesman with a refrigerator truck full of freezer-burned steaks he needed to sell to make his quota and pretend no one was home.

I recognized the short red hair and dorky glasses right away. It was my brother Rowan. I sighed. Although the bark was gone, I had bruises up and down my arms. On top of that, I had a swollen nose and two black eyes from when the rock troll had thrown me into the fence. If Rowan saw me like this, he was totally going to get all Doctor Everlee on me. He knocked again.

"Iris," he shouted. "Are you home?"

I hated ignoring my brother, but I played all the conversations out in my head as to why I looked like I got jumped in an alley. All of them ended with him calling the police on my behalf. I didn't want any cops sniffing around my property because what I had hidden in the backyard was a total stink bomb. At least I didn't stink anymore. After I bathed —twice--in the concoction Keir had suggested, I no longer smelled like troll guts.

"Iris!" He knocked harder.

*Damn it, man, get a clue*! I'd known when I'd asked him to order the drug screen for me two days ago that he'd worry. I could only imagine where his mind would go thinking I'd been drugged and beaten. Unfortunately, he wasn't going away.

My phone rang. Crap. I went to retrieve it from the kitchen. It was Rowan, of course. And now he'd probably heard my phone ring, giving him even more evidence I was home.

I looked around my kitchen and considered escaping out the back to hide in the garden, but I knew that would be the next place Rowan went when I didn't answer my phone. I saw the essential oils, lavender and tea tree next to the peppermint oil I'd used for the clarification spell. Linda had said lavender and tea tree were both excellent for healing wounds. Did bruises count? I hoped so.

I knew the oils should be diluted, but I was desperate as I dotted each onto my arms, chest, neck, and face. I focused my intention. I didn't want my brother to worry about me. I didn't want him mixed up in any of this magic business. I wanted him and the rest of the people I cared about safe. The only way that was happening was for me to get my crap under control.

"Lavender and tea tree, listen to me-me." I rolled my eyes at my terrible rhyme as I continued to dab the oils on my skin. "To be perfectly clear, for the people I care, make these bruises disappear." It wasn't Shakespeare, but I hoped it would do.

A knock at my back window startled me, and I dropped the tea tree bottle on the tile. Some of the oil shot out of the tip, but the amber glass didn't break. *Whew*.

"Iris," my brother said, obvious concern on his face. "Let me in."

I grimaced. How was I going to explain my face and arms? Since hiding wasn't an option, I unlocked the back door and let him in. I waited for his million questions, but he only asked one.

"Why does it stink in here?"

Crap on a candle. Could he smell the troll guts? I'd tried Keir remedy, and I thought it had worked. Had I just acclimated? I mean, it happened. Michael never thought his room smelled like a cesspit.

"I...well. You see there was this skunk and—"

"Skunk? When did skunks start smelling like lavender and antiseptic?"

Ohhh. He'd sniffed out the essential oils. "I heard they were good for stress," I told him. He hadn't said anything about the bruises, even though, when I looked at my reflection in the window, I could still see them. Weird. "So, bro, what brings you by?"

My brother was not a tall man. He only stood about five-eight, a few inches taller than me. His dark hair was thinning, the lines around his eyes had deepened over the years, and he had a cute little tummy pooch. My sisters and I would give the Buddha a pat on family poker nights. It drove Rowan nuts, but we thought it was funny. He was also one of the sweetest men on the planet. Which is why the severe look of concern on his face worried me.

He pushed his glasses up his nose. "Iris, I got your blood work back, and I need to talk to you about the results."

I'd already stopped thinking I'd been drugged, but if he was here personally to bring me bad news, maybe there'd been some merit to my initial beliefs. "What did you find? Was it LSD? PCP? Tell me."

"The drug panels, blood and urine, came back clean."

"Well, that's a relief. I don't see the problem then."

He sighed. "I'm sorry. I was worried about you, so I sent an order to the hospital lab to also do a complete chemical profile on your blood and urinalysis along with the drug screens."

I narrowed my eyes on him. "Ro, that's not what I asked you for."

"You told me you thought you might have accidentally been drugged. You've had a wretched year, and I was concerned about you. I talked to Dahlia—"

"You what?" Anger thinned my lips. "You had no right, Rowan."

"I know, but I'm your brother, and I'm worried about you. We all are."

Apparently, my siblings had been holding Iris Meetings behind my back. "I'm excellent," I lied. Because I was anything but. "I don't need you all butting in. I mean, I love you, but this is my life." I'd heard the expression "blood boiling mad" before, but as my body burned with anger, I finally understood the term. "If that's all. You can go."

He lowered his gaze. "That's not all." He gestured to my kitchen table. "I think you need to sit down for this."

Bob vaulted to the counter and bumped me with his head.

Rowan didn't comment on the cat, so I knew his news must be dire. "Is it cancer?"

He shook his head. "I honestly don't know. I've never seen anything like this before, Iris. I want to start by retesting your blood."

"What did you find?"

"First, your white blood cell count is through the roof.

Have you been running fevers this past week?" He reached out and touched my forehead with the back of his hand. "You feel hot right now."

"That's rage," I told him.

He frowned and arched his brow. "Your lymphocytes, monocytes, and your basophils are a hundred times the normal limit. Your body is fighting against something really hard."

*Magic,* I thought. *My body is fighting the magic.* No wonder I felt like crap, other than the obvious troll beat down.

"Even more concerning is your chemical profile. The calcium in your blood is high, which can signify heart disease. Your potassium levels, magnesium levels, and sodium levels are something I've never seen before. I couldn't even find a single illness or disease that would cause all these to be so elevated."

Everything he'd listed off was minerals, like the kind you find in the Earth. My stomach sank. This had to be what happened to a body as wild Earth magic took over. It was burning me up. The extra minerals were the beginning of dust. Even with my successful spells yesterday, I hadn't really mastered a damn thing, had I? The results were looking pretty conclusive. The super moon and lunar eclipse was tomorrow night, and I was going to end up a pile of ash for the rest of the magic world to divide into lines and snort right up.

"Someone had to screw up the tests," I said. "I feel great." I stretched my arms up, trying to hide my grimace of pain. It must have worked because Rowan didn't seem to notice.

"I want you to get tested again."

"Come on. With those numbers, I'd probably be dead already, right?"

The tension around his eyes didn't ease, but he nodded. "That's true. But still. I'd feel better if you would just do them again."

"Fine," I said. "You order them, and I'll go in on Tuesday and take the tests."

"Why not tomorrow?" he asked.

"I have plans tomorrow that I can't cancel." Dust Day was nearly upon me. "If I start feeling bad, I'll go to the emergency room, okay?" I hoped my tone was calm and reassuring because the voice in my brain was anything but. "And speaking of plans, I have to get ready. I'm meeting a friend."

"A guy friend?" my brother asked.

"Seriously, Ro. Not you too."

"I checked in with Michael yesterday." I knew that he and Rowan talked occasionally. I was glad my brother had stepped up for my son when he didn't feel comfortable talking to his father or me. "He says you are doing some freelance editing for some guy that was here at the house on Friday. Then Marigold told me it was for her friend. Keir Quinn?" He said Keir's name as if it was a question.

"Yes, yeah," I said. "I have to go to his place to nail down the details of the contract. It's a good gig, though."

Rowan, after a few more minutes of reassurance that I would redo the tests and that I would call him or go to the emergency room if I got as much as a splinter, left.

And so, I wouldn't be a complete liar, I called Keir.

He answered on the first ring. "I'm in town," he said. "I can swing by and get you."

I nodded numbly. So much had happened in the last four

days, from the divorce to finding out I was a witch who might die, dealing with ex-husband BS, killing a troll, and now, proof that my body was failing me.

He must've seen my decision in one of his visions because he said, "I'll be at your house in five."

## CHAPTER 19

THE OVER-THE-COUNTER PAIN RELIEVERS HAD FINALLY kicked in about the time we arrived at Keir's tiny house. After he parked, I got out and walked down to the rocky falls in his backyard, hugging my bruised arms.

Yes, they were still bruised, along with my nose and eyes. I didn't know why my brother hadn't noticed, but I didn't want to look a gift horse in the mouth. Although, frankly, the gift horse could've just gotten rid of the bruises like I asked. I thought about what Rowan had said with the white blood cells. The areas of elevation were acting as if my body was treating the wild terra-craft magic coursing through my veins like an allergy or a virus. I'd been running hot since the night before, but after Rowan left, I'd taken my temperature. 102.9. Not good. Linda had said wild magic would burn in me. The blonde druid woman had said the wild magic would choke everything in its path. I was beginning to think they were both right. The high mineral count. The fever. It was all a symptom of one thing. This world was about to kiss my ash.

I couldn't believe just five days ago, I'd thought my biggest problem was going to be moving on with my life after Evan. My ex-cheater was still a concern, but not in the same way. If something happened to me, Michael would be stuck with Evan. Did I think Evan loved our son? Absolutely. Did I think he was selfish for putting his own desires above his family's? Yep, that was true too. Which is why I worried that he might not step up if I died. Michael would be okay, though, right? He had my dad, my sisters, and my brother to look out for him and only one more year of high school to get through.

"Can I beat this?" I asked Keir when he walked up and stood beside me.

"Yes," he said.

"You've seen that future?" I asked.

"No." He picked up a stone and tossed it into the stream. "Things have been...fuzzy lately. It's as if I can see a thousand possibilities leading up to tomorrow night's lunar eclipse. Still, no matter what choice you make, I can't see the outcome."

"Not a single one?"

He shook his head. "I'm sorry."

"I guess it's a done deal then. If you can't see my future, Keir, then it means I don't have one."

"I refuse to believe that." He rubbed the star-shaped scar on his wrist. "I won't believe it." He clenched his fists. I watched his knuckles blanch white from the effort.

I reached over and put my hand on his. Slowly, almost

reluctantly, he opened his hands. His palms were bloody where his nails had dug in. I laced my fingers with his.

Keir had said he was bonded to me. That I was his purpose. If I was gone, would he be there for Michael? I hoped so. Almost as much for Keir's sake. I knew what it was like to be a mother. To feel a devotion to another human being that will last me until the day I die. The way Keir had explained his "calling" reminded me of that kind of devotion. If anything ever happened to Michael, I…I didn't know how I'd stand this world. I didn't want that for Keir. It wasn't his fault he'd been magically screwed by fate. If I couldn't fight the burn, I needed to know he'd be okay.

"Is there a spell or something that can break your connection to me?"

He clenched his jaw and turned his steeling gaze on it. "Don't even think about it, Iris."

"It's not fair to you—"

He cut me off. "If you try to sever the bond, it will be a betrayal of my existence."

"But if we could make it as if that tie between us never existed, then you would be free. You won't have to experience the pain of my failure."

"Or the joy of your success," he added.

"That too," I agreed. "But it's not looking good for me, pal."

"Is anything easy ever worthwhile?"

I snorted a laugh. "Absolutely. Easy is the best." Oh, how I longed for easy. But life seldom gave you want you wanted. I thought of my mother and her predicament. She might have had a terminal diagnosis, but we hadn't expected her to pass so quickly. On one hand, I'd been thankful she hadn't had to suffer long. On the other hand, I hadn't gotten to say my goodbye, no closure between us at the end of her final chapter. I'd often wondered what we would have done differently, or what she would have done differently, if we had known she only had one more day to live.

"If you knew you only had one night to live, what would you do with it?" I asked.

He stared far off as if he could see past the horizon. "I don't know," he finally said. "What would you do?"

I smiled, even as an extreme chill rushed through me, and I began to shiver. "I know the romantic answer would be to find some hot guy to sleep with and fall madly in love, but that's fairy tales, and this is real life." Keir was sexy enough for the hot guy part, and as to falling madly in love, I cared about him, but I wasn't sure the "in love" part was possible overnight. "This isn't a fairytale, and I'm not some damsel in distress who is content to do nothing while I wait to be rescued. Because, if my rescue never comes, then what? So, if this is my last night, I want to spend it with the people I care about. My dad, my sisters, my brother, my son, Bob, Linda, and you."

Keir chuckled. "I'm glad I made it on the list, even if I did come after the imp and the gnome." He turned to face me and brought my knuckles to his lips. "I have faith in you, Iris. I believe you will face the test and survive it. But if you want tonight to be family night. Then I am on board one hundred percent. Like I told you before, I got your back." He grinned and wrapped his arms around me. If possible, I felt even colder.

"Nerd," I said. I glanced at the bruises on my shoulders. "What about these?"

He let me go and looked at my arms. "These?" The question hung between us for a few seconds.

"My upper body looks like I went ten rounds with Mike Tyson back when he was biting ears off."

Keir frown as he stared down at me. His dark hair fell forward over his eyes. "I don't see any bruises, Iris."

I lifted my arms. "How can you not see this?" The entire spectrum of purples was visible from my hands to my shoulders. "Or this?" I pointed to my face. "I'd give Rocket Raccoon a run for his money when it came to black eyes."

"Honestly, you look...beautiful. I was surprised when I first saw you because I was sure last night when I left you that you would be a mess today. But you appear none the worse for wear."

Oh, man. I was definitely worse for wear. Had I done another screwy incantation? "When my brother came by this morning, I tried to cast a healing spell."

"Okay," Keir said. "Did anything happen?"

"I thought it hadn't because I can still see the battering my body took. But Rowan didn't freak out. I thought it was strange, but then he told me the results of my blood panel, and my appearance seemed the least of my troubles." The chill in the air was getting more severe. "Did the te-te-temperature just dr-dr-drop forty degrees?" My teeth chattered. "I'm so cold."

Keir cupped my face. "You are burning up, Iris."

"I...I had a fe-fe-fever earlier."

"I think you still do." He put his arm around me. "I'm taking you home."

"M'k-ka-kay." As we walked to the car, my skin buzzed as

if electrified. Great, I was burning, freezing, and frying. And it wasn't even Dust Day! "I...I don't feel r-r-right."

A loud screech echoed off the rock cliff wall, and a great, gray-winged creature came swooping down on Keir and me.

My frozen limbs and my fever-addled brain thought I was having another hallucination until I Keir threw us both to the ground and hissed, "Gargoyle."

"Wha-at?" A gargoyle? I'd just fought off a troll the day before. I'd used all the energy in my body, and I wasn't sure I had the strength in me to defeat another creature. Besides, Linda hadn't mentioned anything about gargoyles. My eyes grew big as I watched the beast with a wingspan at least eight feet wide claw at Keir's back. The pain in his face as he kept me covered and protected was too much to bear. "Don't..." I tried to shove him away, but he bracketed me with his arms and legs, his face inches from mine. "Save yourself," I said.

Tears crystallized in his gray eyes as he stared down at me. "Protecting you is how I save myself." His voice was low, hollow, and inhuman. "Close your eyes, Iris," he said through gritted teeth. I don't want you to see this."

Only, I couldn't look away. However, I was not prepared for what happened next. Dark brown fur sprouted over Keir's cheeks as he roared when the gargoyle sunk its claws into his back. Then my gentle druid's mouth widened, and his teeth became hideous fangs. His ears elongated, moving up his scalp to the top of his head, and his eyes turn pitch black. Sharp antlers, five points each shot from the top of his skull, and his arms had grown to the size of tree trunks. He stared down at me, saliva dripping from his frightening maw. He lifted one hand from the ground, and out of his fingertips were claws that looked as if they were made of black diamonds. He reached over his shoulder and ripped the gargoyle away, throwing the stone beast a good twenty feet.

Whatever Keir had turned into, stood at its full height taller than the troll, so over ten feet, and about as wide. He turned his attention to the gargoyle, and in one ferocious leap, he was on our attacker. He ripped off the wings as if the stony monster was nothing more than a fly, and then he plunged his terrible claws deep into the gargoyle's heart and pulled it straight out its chest. The fever blurred my vision, but within seconds Keir was back. My Keir, not the thing he'd turned into. He was cradling me. "Are you okay? Did he hurt you?"

I shook my head. "What?"

"I'll explain later," he said. He picked me up and carried me to his car. Gently he put me in the back seat and covered me with a light blanket. "Rest now, Iris. I'll get you help. I promise."

I patted his cheek. "And you keep your promises."

He smiled down at me. "I surely do."

## CHAPTER 20

I DREAMED OF BEASTLY BUNNIES WITH LONG EARS AND short tails, giant antlers and fangy teeth. In other words, Stephen King's version of Alice in Wonderland. Only, instead of the rabbit being late, he was ripping the heart out of the Queen of Hearts and her entire deck of soldiers.

I jolted awake to the beep-beep-beep of a nearby machine. I was in a white room, in a strange, uncomfortable bed, oxygen tubing up my nose, and an IV stuck in my arm. Okay. This was definitely the hospital, but things were still a little fuzzy on the how.

"She's awake," I heard someone say. Seconds later, my son walked in looking more worried than I'd ever seen him. I couldn't stop the tears from clouding my vision as he gave me a quick hug. My dad, a large man with gray hair and the biggest capacity for love, followed behind him. Then, Rose and her husband Don, their boys Drake and Dustin, my oldest sister Dahlia, Marigold, and Rowan. And right at the back, carrying a suspiciously familiar duffle bag, was Keir.

My energy was low, but I managed to smile as each one gave me a kiss hello.

When it was Keir's turn, he set the bag down, then leaned over and kissed my cheek. "You said you wanted a family night."

"Not like this." I touched his arm. "But I'll take it."

My dad was talking loudly, ordering my siblings about. Telling people to give me space. Then he sat down on the edge of my bed, and he held my hand. "You gave us quite the scare there, girly."

"Sorry, Dad."

He patted my cheek. "How come you didn't tell me you weren't feeling well?"

"It came on suddenly, Dad. I didn't know I was getting sick. Honest."

"Well, you're getting help now. That's what counts." His almost colorless blue eyes were red and watery. I'd really scared him. Losing Mom, his one great love had been hard for him, though I'm sure he still hadn't gotten over it. I knew it was killing him to see me like this, but he put on a brave face for his children, though.

"I'm glad you're here."

"Me too, kiddo."

Before he could move away, I tugged him back. "I love you, Dad."

A strange look passed across his face, but he shook it off. "I love you, too."

Rowan went into Dr. Everlee mode. "You had a fever of over 106.2 when your friend brought you into the emergency room. Luckily, the nurse on duty recognized your name and called me."

"Luckily," I said with a wan smile. Michael made a choking sound that broke my heart. I'd really scared him. "I'm okay, babe," I said, but it was hard to convince him when I was on oxygen and hooked up to an IV.

Rowan gave me a look of frustration. "If you had listened to me this morning—"

"You're right," I said to head off any arguing. I didn't want to debate the merits of modern medicine in the treatment of mystical ailments. "I should have gone to the hospital earlier."

My concession mollified him some. "We managed to get the fever down with anti-fever meds, a cooling blanket, and the IV to get your hydration up. But you still have a low-grade fever. We're running more tests to see if you have an infection. But the doctor put you on an antibiotic as prophylaxis. You know, to treat any infections you have or that might develop. If we get lucky, it could have you back on your feet in no time."

I waved for my brother to come over to me. When he was standing next to me, I rubbed his belly. "There, that's all the good luck I need."

He flicked me on the nose. "Knucklehead."

I leaned my head back on my pillow and closed my eyes. Damn, I was tired. Rose, as usual, took charge. "Okay," she said. "Everybody out. Iris needs her rest." She moved Rowan out of the way and hugged me. "I'll take care of Michael," she said. "Don't you worry about him? You concentrate on getting better, you hear me?"

Emotion choked me. "Thank you," I croaked as I fought back the tears again.

"Leave it to Rose to bring the temperature of a room

down," Marigold teased. She, like me, used humor in stressful situations. But she went in for another hug as well and whispered, "See, I told you Keir was a keeper."

"You actually said he was hot."

She wiggled her brows. "Same thing. Get better. I can't be the only sister who knows how to have fun."

"You got it."

Dahlia, the oldest and the most stoic of the bunch, was wearing a velvet tracksuit. Her favorite leisurewear. She'd let her hair gray naturally, and she had a beautiful silver streak on one side that gave her an air of sophistication that she totally owned. "I love you," she said simply.

Tears wet my eyes again. "Damn you, Dahlia."

She smiled. That awesome bitch knew exactly what she was doing when it came to heart-string tugging. "I'll see you later."

I nodded. "Yep."

Don and the boys left after Rose, and my dad and Michael went home shortly after that.

"You be good," I told Michael.

"I will," he said.

"You know I love you, and I'm so proud of you. You are the best son a mother could want."

"Mom," he said my name like a complaint as he wiped his eyes. "I love you too."

"I know you do. I never doubt it."

My dad put his arm around Michael, and they left, leaving Rowan and Keir. I gave my brother a sideways glance. "Can you give me a minute with Keir?"

"Uh, sure," Rowan said. "Yep. I'll be out in the hall."

"Hey, Ro?"

"Yeah," he replied.

"Thanks for looking out for me."

"That's what big brothers do." He opened the door, gave it a quick pat, and exited.

"I don't think your brother likes me," Keir said when we were alone.

"If you think I was so delirious that I don't remember you turning into vampire-bunny-alope with gnarly claws and teeth, you are sadly mistaken." I kept my tone light because I wasn't mad at him. Did it freak me out? A bit, yeah. But if he hadn't turned into whatever he turned into, we both would've died.

He lifted the duffle bag up and said, "What if I give you what's in this bag as a bribe for you to let this one go?"

The reason the bag looked familiar was because it was mine. The last time I'd used it was for an overnight work trip. "I don't care what's in the bag. I need to know what you are."

He pinched the zipper and opened it up. An impishly impish imp popped his adorably chubby face out of the opening.

I bit back a cry. "Bob!"

"Shhh," Keir said. "No animals on the premises unless they are licensed support animals."

"Bob isn't licensed, but he should be bottled and sold as a cure for the blues." I hugged my snuggly cuddle monkey. "I love you, Bob." In the same breath, I said to Kier, "This doesn't get you out of an explanation."

He sighed. Heavily. "I told you that I had to do some things before I could take on the commitment of our bond. This," he spread his hands wide, "was that thing. My sacrifice in order to be strong enough to fight beside you. Otherwise, I would've been a liability."

"Just spit it out, man," I said in a baby-talk voice as I scratched Bob's back right in front of his twitchy, nubby tail.

"I'm a puca."

"A pooh who?"

Keir closed his eyes and grimaced. "A shapeshifter. I can turn into animals."

"And one scary-ass monster."

"Yes," he agreed, "that too."

"What, you can turn into other animals?" I thought about the long-eared rabbit that had taken a particular interest in my garden since spring. "Have you been spying on me?"

He frowned. "I like to think of it as watching out for you, but..."

I giggled. "I forgive you. Especially since you saved my life. What there is left of it."

He gave me a worried look. "Iris..."

"Don't." I pressed my palm against his cheek. "Thank you for protecting me."

He nodded. "You're welcome."

"Soooo, is the future any clearer? Did getting me to the hospital fix anything?"

"I still can't see past right now, but you're alive. That's something, right?"

"It is." I stroked Bob's fur as he curled up on my stomach. "Thanks for bringing, Bob. He's the best medicine."

Keir grinned. "It's how he's made."

"I know." I gave him an irritated glance. "And I don't care. We all have something, Mr. Puca."

Rowan stuck his head in the room. "Visiting hours are over. You need to recover your strength."

"And the brother had spoken," Keir teased me after Rowan closed the door.

"What am I going to do tomorrow? If this is how my magic is behaving the day before this mystical timebomb event, I'm scared."

Keir sat down on the bed next to me and placed his palm on the left side of my chest. "As long as this beats, there's hope. And I'm not going to stop fighting for you until there is nothing more to fight for."

He'd said the bond was such that he would give his life for mine, and now his words scared me so much. "Promise me you won't try to sacrifice yourself for me."

The corner of his mouth tugged into a half-smile. "I don't make promises I can't keep." There was a moment when I thought he'd lean over and kiss me, but a rapid knock on the door put an end to it.

"Rowan is such a buzzkill," I said.

Keir's gray eyes flickered toward the door then back to me. Then, without fanfare, he dipped his head, and with only the slightest hesitation, his lips met mine. It was soft at first, just a gentle brush of mouth against mouth, but then the pressure became a little more insistent. *Whew*. Talk about intention. The sizzle from the kiss was electrifying, so much so, I almost looked around for another gargoyle attack.

When he finished, I blinked up into those gorgeous gray eyes. "That was...unexpected."

He grinned mischievously and winked at me. "I saw it coming."

# CHAPTER 21

A NURSE HAD SEEN BOB AND HAD GIVEN HIM TO KEIR TO take home. She'd warned him he'd be banned if he brought the cat back—what a bee-otch. I really had a lot of respect for the profession, but anyone who could take one look at Bob and not melt, well, that was a person I didn't want to know.

My fever spiked again at midnight. D-Day. It rose to 104.2. The nurse pushed IV paracetamol to bring it down, but it held steady. That's when they brought the cooling blanket in. Thank heavens I'd been passed out the first time they'd used it because this felt like actual torture.

A blonde nurse came in wearing a surgical mask, a cap, and a gown. Did they think I was contagious?

"I'm going to take you for a treatment, Ms. Everlee. Doctor's orders." She yanked up the rails on my bed, unhooked the IV bag from the pole, and hung it on a hook at the top of the hospital bed. The earlier nurse had put me back on oxygen. This one took it off.

"What kind of treatment?" I asked.

"It's something that will help manage your pain," she said.

My fevered brain registered something was wrong—off—about the nurse. But I couldn't figure out what it was. Even so, I wanted pain relief. Every muscle, every nerve fiber, even my hair hurt.

When we got on the elevator, she took down her mask. She had scars on her face that I recognized, but I wondered if my fever was sending my brain bad signals. I narrowed my gaze at her.

"I know you."

"Yes, Iris, you do, and we don't have much time."

"You're Blondie the Boss Bitch." Of course, I still might have been experiencing a fevered delusion. I mean, just because the first time had been real doesn't mean this time was.

The woman smiled. "Yes. And I'm going to help you."

"Oh, okay." The idea of help was grand. I just wished she'd hurry up and do whatever she was going to do. Hell, I think I would've taken a knock in the head at this point. I started perspiring profusely as if all the liquid was leaving my body. "Sweaty," I said. "Drenched."

"Your fever's breaking," she explained.

"That's nice." I gave her a lazy smile. "Where are we going?"

"I can't let you turn to dust in a hospital bed. There would be too many questions."

I nodded. "That makes sense." I reached out and stroked her hand. "Ouch." The contact had been like raking my fingers over hot coals or acid. In other words, it burned. Keir had said he believed in me. Linda, maybe she believed in me. Bob, he was my cuddly, yummy-num-num. I craned my head back so I could look at Blondie.

"Do you think I'm going to die?" I asked her.

She smiled down at me as she shoved the bed out of the elevator and into a carport. "I'm counting on it."

I blinked. "What?" My limbs felt numb, and my eyes felt heavy. "Did you do something to me?"

"Just added propofol and fentanyl in your paracetamol." She winked. "It'll paralyze you for a short time and keep you nice and docile, so I can transfer you to a safe spot, but it'll wear off soon enough."

"Safe for who?"

"For me, of course." She gestured with her hand for someone to come over. And two someones, both men, unhooked me from the IV and moved me out of bed. They shoved my useless body into the back of a cargo van.

I was scared, angry, and my veins were on fire. Also, the stupid hospital gown I was in was up around my waist. "Will someone at least cover my ass?"

"Drive," Blondie said to one of her henchmen. She threw a blanket over me. "Don't worry, Iris. This will all be over for you soon."

I concentrated on moving my fingers. If I could move even one, I told myself, then I would find a way out of this. I knew my chances of surviving, let alone escaping, were slim, but little victories might keep me from losing my mind. "Why are you doing this? You're a druid. I thought you were on my side?"

One of the men chuckled. That was never good.

"I'm going to share you with my cabal. Your Earth magic

is something we haven't seen in—well, ever. How someone so wild in her terra-craft managed to tear apart a rock troll...that's going to be the stuff of legends, honey."

"Cabal? You are really going all in on the movie villain stereotype." My pinky finger twitched. I celebrated on the inside because the outside of me was still ninety-nine-point-nine percent not functional. "And don't call me honey, honey," I added, just because I hated it when people I didn't know—especially assholes who drugged and kidnapped me—called me things like honey, sugar, sweetie, or darling. Friends or family, totally cool. Strangers and psychopathic druids could suck it.

And oh my, gosh! My big toe wiggled.

The sweat was dripping off me now. The carpet under me was soaked. This didn't feel like a normal fever breaking. "What's wrong with me?" My tongue was so dry it kept sticking to the roof of my mouth. "I need water," I croaked.

"She's accelerating," Blondie said. "Drive faster."

My other fingers started to move. They were stiff, but the movement was progressing. I wasn't sure what I would accomplish with one toe and five fingers, but I needed the win. The skin on my face and arms began to tighten down as if squeezing my bones. I wasn't panicking, and I didn't know why. Was I frightened? Totally. Did I want to die? No way. But instead of out of my head scared, I was super chill. What is it the blond nutjob had said? *Propofol and fentanyl in your paracetamol.*

Oh, right. Fentanyl. My guess was I was high enough to take the edge off but not so high as to be unaware of what was happening to me. Deep down, I really wished she'd given me a much bigger dose. "Water," I said again.

"You're starting to mummify." Blondie smiled. "Did you know that the human body is made up of sixty percent water?"

"Duh, I had to take life science in school like everyone else." I'm sure my sarcasm had been impossible to read since my words were raspy and barely audible. The skin on my neck constricted, and it felt like I was wearing a turtleneck five sizes too small for me. Is this what turning to ash was like? All the liquid leaves the body, and the organic parts of you dry up and poof. Dust.

I was still confused by Keir's boss's evil behavior, though. I was sure the druids were the good guys, right? But this one had her own cabal. Is that what a druid circle was called? Why didn't I ask more questions? Maybe because my life had been one reaction after another since this mystical crap-show had started.

Was this it? Was this how it ended? At least, I'd seen everyone I loved and told them how I felt. I'd said goodbye. That meant something, right?

The van jostled to a stop. "We're here," one of the dudes said.

"Get her out," the blonde directed. "Put her on the altar."

I think the water loss cleared some of the fentanyl from my system because my entire body screamed with pain before I went completely numb. My head cleared enough for me to panic. Linda had warned me about Earth elementals, but the people she said were the most dangerous to me were *the Hexenmeister*.

Aw, damn it. Boss bitch was a sorcerer. She had to be. Linda had said there was no way to detect one unless they used their borrowed power. Surely, Keir would have known if she was a baddie. Had the blonde druid been hiding her gifts this whole time? Or did she decide that being a druid wasn't enough, and she wanted a witch's power for herself. Was I to be her first sacrifice?

The two men carried me log-style to the altar. My leg bone snapped. I heard it. I saw it dangling. But I still couldn't feel it. The magic flaming through me must have short-circuited my pain receptors. The guys dropped me hard on the stone altar. This one wasn't white like I'd seen with the druid circle. Instead, this one was yellow marble. I could see some of the runes, but like before, I didn't know what they meant. If I had do-overs, I'd make Keir teach me everything he knew about this stuff so I wouldn't be caught unawares again.

The blonde's cabal, as she called her group, was made up of what seemed like a dozen men and women in red cowls. Were they serious? Did they shop for clothes at Villains R Us?

"Are you sure there's enough of me to go around? I'm more of a snack than a family dinner kind of meal." My voice was more of a dry hiss than anything with a tone, so I'm not sure she heard me, but a woman in a red robe laughed.

Blondie stood over me, her arms held out wide. "The time is near. She's almost dust, my brothers and sisters. After tonight, we shall no longer be protectors of the witches' powers, we will be the powerful. And with this Earth sacrifice, we will begin the journey to claim our strength for the fight that is yet to come."

Yet to come? I remembered Linda or Keir or someone talking about a larger threat down the road. Were they the weapons, and I was the ammunition? And were the other members of Blondie's cabal druids, as well. Keir was so noble and true in his commitment to me, that I hadn't even imagined that any of the druids could be corrupt.

I wished Keir was here. His evil antlered rabbit form would take these assholes down in a flash. But he wasn't. It was me. I only had myself to rely on, and *myself* could have been an extra on any one of the Mummy movies. The Brendan Frasier ones, of course.

I guess the high mineral counts in my bloodwork had all been leading up to this moment. Soon, I would be a magical chum for the circling sorcerers.

If only I had ingredients. I could weave a spell. It might or might not work, but at least I would go out knowing I'd tried.

I wanted to be free of these witch-wannabe jerks, but four days had not been a lot of time to learn how to defend myself. One by one, the *Hexenmeister* approached. Each one of them placed a single kiss on my forehead. I tried hissing at them, but my lungs were barely functioning. The one who laughed lifted her cowl slightly so I could see her face.

Shock and rage churned inside me. Luanne Danvers. I had liked her, damn it. We were going out for dancing and drinks. No. I couldn't believe she was one of those *hexen-idiots*. She gave me a little wink, and if I could have punched her in the face, I would have with pleasure.

I would kill her. I would kill them all for this. The rage sharpened my mind, but it also brought back some of the pain. *Good*, I thought. *The pain lets me know I'm alive*.

Did I have herbs and spices? Nope. But I wasn't entirely without earth ingredients. I called on the calcium, sodium, potassium, magnesium, and whatever other was left in me to do my bidding. I was a witch. I had the spark of tru-craft, not these thieves, and I was not going down without a fight.

I couldn't vocalize my incantation, so I mouthed it. "Make me whole, muscle to muscle, bone to bone, make my flesh from bits of stone."

There was no surge of power. Argh. I wanted my body back so I can make these *hexen-bitches* pay. I mouthed it again. "Make me whole, muscle to muscle, bone to bone, make my flesh from bits of stone."

Blondie must have seen my lips moving because she leaned down. "No time for last words," she said. "It'll be over soon."

"For you," I hissed. Oh. Progress. "Make me whole, muscle to muscle, bone to bone, make my flesh from bits of stone." The energy inside me surged, finally. Triumphantly, I added, "Give me strength to stand alone in this body built of stone. Let me bring my enemies down, especially this stupid blonde clown."

Blondie blanched as I sat up.

"Strap her down," she said, staggering away from me. I reached into the soil around me, looking for anything to use as a weapon. Then I found the perfect tool. Wild morning glory, also known as bindweed. Let's see how she liked being choked out by wild magic.

The ground began to shake as tendrils of thin, thread-like vines erupted from the grass.

The blonde's shocked expression was almost as good as the screams from her cabal as the weeds did my bidding.

Then she turned and ran.

# CHAPTER 22

My body felt stiff as I got to my feet. I was impressed by the way the terra-craft had fixed my broken leg. And I was no longer in blinding pain or dying of thirst. I stood on the altar and aimed my magic at the cabal. "Binding, winding, growing strong. Do my bidding. Undo this wrong."

The vines yanked the cabal down one by one. Apparently, I was decent at terra-craft as long as I was pissed off. That seemed to be when it worked the best.

"Bind and wind, choke them out. Make them scream. Make them shout."

Red-robed bodies writhed on the ground as the vines tightened around them, holding them hostage.

Luanne howled as she threw off her bad-guy costume. Under her robe, she was dressed in military black, and she was strapped up with knives and guns. She wore a bulletproof vest.

A howl in the distance answered back. Did I want to

know what was coming? Probably not. I tried to stand, but legs made of minerals didn't move so fast.

Luanne leaped through the air like a ninja warrior on steroids, with her knife held aloft, and I readied my magic. If I could crack a troll like an egg, she wouldn't be too difficult to dispatch. Right? Her fierce cry gave me pause as she landed next to me and aimed the blade downward —behind me.

I whipped around and saw one of Blondie's henchmen drop an actual freaking scythe. Lu's dagger had plunged into his neck, and he grabbed at the blade as he fell to the ground.

"I'm with Keir," she said. "He's on his way. Can you move?"

I nodded. "I think so." I still wasn't sure I could trust Luanne, but I wanted to. I wanted to believe that I wasn't alone. Because the worst part of the painless nothing had been the knowledge that I would die surrounded by strangers and not the people I loved.

As the bindweed sought out members of Blondie's cabal, the red robed assholes who weren't already bound, scrambled to their feet and scattered.

Luanne jumped down, throwing up her arm as a guy tried to strike her with a mace. She dropped down and nailed him in the nuts with an uppercut. It worked better for her against the man than it had for me with the troll, and the guy went down. I used my power to tie him up with the weeds.

I climbed down off the altar. My magic pulsed through me, a living thing that obeyed me without question. I felt powerful. Like I could take on the whole world.

"Another one bites the dust," Luanne said. "Get it?" She was having way too much fun considering I had almost died, and she hadn't done a damn thing to help. Still, I could appreciate the enthusiasm. "Where did Bogmall go?" she asked.

I shrugged. I'd forgotten the blonde was named Bogmall. "She took off when I...you know, fixed myself."

Luanne laughed. "Yeah, you did." She held up her hand for a high five.

I left her hanging. Much the way she had left me hanging on the altar.

"Aww, come on," Luanne said, following me as I made sure every *hexen-dick* that hadn't managed to escape was bound. Tightly. "You can't be mad at me. I was here to help you."

"Some help."

"Look, there wasn't a thing I could if you couldn't get your magic under control. Jumping in sooner would have just gotten us both dead."

She wasn't wrong. But I still wasn't ready to let her off the hook. I scoured the surroundings, searching for Bogmall. "Are you a sorcerer?" I asked.

"Oh, hell, no," she said. "I just play one on TV." She raised her hand. "Kidding. I'm a druid, like Keir. I followed you up here from the hospital. Parked my motorcycle about a mile down the road. Found one of these pissants taking a leak. Stabbed 'em, stole their bathrobe, bing, bang, boom. Bob's your uncle."

"Bob's my imp."

"You know what I mean. Anyway, I called Keir as soon as I got on the road, but the cell phone reception is non-existent out here. I'm pretty sure he's coming in all warrior Puca."

"You know about his..." I hissed then made a scary bunny face.

"For a while now," she said. "But I only started working with Keir about five years ago after I got out of the service."

"So, you didn't take a class from me eighteen years ago?"

"Nah," Lu said. "But I bet you would've been a blast.

I shook my head. "I don't know about that." I wondered about her connection with Keir. He must trust her if she knew his secret. "How long have you known him? Keir, I mean."

Before she could answer, an Earth-shattering roar preceded several trees getting knocked down as a giant Puca ran out of the woods.

When its black eyes locked on mine, it dropped down to all fours and sprinted the rest of the way to my location. When it was in front of me, it...he changed. Within seconds, I was staring into those gorgeous gray eyes.

"You're alive," he said.

"Mostly." I picked leaves from his hair.

Luanne turned away from us. "Gross, Keir. You need to start carrying a backpack. She grabbed the robe she'd discarded. "Here."

He chuckled as he put it on. He glanced at Luanne then back to me. "I see you've met my sister."

I don't know why the news relieved me, but it did. I wanted to be mad that he hadn't told me sooner, but really, we'd known each other for less than a week.

I clenched my fist. "Do I feel hard to you?"

"That's what he said," Luanne smirked.

I laughed. "You're terrible."

"You'll come to love that about me."

I grinned at her. "I'm sure I will." I turned my attention back to Keir. "I made myself out of minerals. I don't feel rigid when I touch it, but I'm worried that I've been gnomified."

He squeezed my forearm. "It's more firm than your normal muscle tone but not rockhard."

I guess that was a consolation.

"Can I kiss you again?"

"You didn't ask permission the last time."

"The last time, I didn't know if I would get another chance."

I raised up on my toes as he leaned down. Our lips met, and wowza, it was magic.

"So, I'm really okay? No more dust?"

"No more dust," Keir said. He kissed me once more.

"We gotta go," Luanne said. "Don't know what happened to Bogmall, but she'll be back."

"Wait, Bogmall did this," Keir said. "She's been the leader of my grove for over ten years."

"Dude." Lu nodded. "Surprised the crap out of me too. When I saw her stuff Iris in the van, it threw me for a loop."

"I'm safe now. And she won't get the upper hand on me again." At least, I hoped not.

Keir caressed my face. "We'll get her."

"Together," I said.

He nodded. "Together. But for now, we need to get you back to the hospital so we can call off the search party."

Luanne glanced around at the trapped sorcerers-in-training. "I'll take care of these yahoos."

I gave her a wary glance. "I don't want to know how, do I?"

She shook her head. "Probably for the best." She tossed some keys to Keir. "These are for the van. Took them off the guy who drove it here."

Keir easily caught the keys. "See you soon."

"Thanks," I told her. Like the gnome, Lu was growing on me. Then I turned to Keir. "You ready?"

Keir held my hand and said, "For whatever comes next."

*Two weeks later...*

"No, *Kleinkind*, not like that," Linda said as she pelted me with another rock. As a side effect of rebuilding myself with my own minerals, it hurt way less than it had before. She clapped her gnomie little hands. "Again."

I couldn't be mad at her. Linda had become a real mentor to me. Besides, when I'd returned home after my hospital stay, she'd sobbed so hard I thought she was going to blow off her winklepickers. Keir and I had come up with a cover story that I'd awoken hungry, my fever gone, and I'd gone in search of food. I'd worried about security videos, but Lu assured me she'd taken care of all that. Keir's sister was funny, pretty, stupidly scary, and we were becoming the best of friends.

I did the blood tests again that my brother wanted, but Lu helped there too. She switched my blood sample with hers before the lab got a hold of it. Low and behold, everything came back normal. My brother was sure I'd had some kind of infection, and the antibiotic I'd gotten in the hospital had fixed it. I was happy for him to believe that.

Everyone in my family had been relieved that I was okay. My dad swore I took five years off his life. I hoped that wasn't true. And Michael. I shook my head. It was five days after I got home before he'd left the house again. My hospitalization had really scared him. Evan still hadn't talked to him about leaving. I swore if that man didn't do right by my kid, I was going to practice a little tru-craft in his direction.

I put my fingertips against a boulder and said, "I am the rock. The rock is me. Don't resist. Let me enter thee." I sunk my fingers to the knuckles. "Look! I did it. I'm fingering the rock." I laughed. It earned me another pebble to the forehead.

Keir walked out the back door. "Cool," he said as I wiggled my free thumb at him.

"I'm pretty sure this was how Arthur's sword got in the stone." I reversed my fingers. And this time, the stone didn't take the top layer of skin. Success!

"Are you ready for dinner?"

"Does she look ready, druid?" Linda asked.

"Can you give me about twenty minutes? I want to write this fingers-in-stone spell down and change clothes."

"Into your good yoga pants?" the gnome asked.

Smart ass. "Shut up, Linda."

"You know the spell has a real name. It's not called fingers-in-rock spell," she chided.

"I'll call it what I want," I shot back. Adding spells to my grimoire had become a source of great joy for me. Every new thing I learned I eagerly wrote it down. Bogmall was gone, but I knew she'd be back. She'd blown up her druid gig to try and steal my magic, and I couldn't see her just giving up. Next time, though, I would be ready for her.

"Sure," Keir said.

"Great!" I skipped up to the house feeling better than I had in such a long time. Keir and I were taking things slow, and I was glad. I wasn't ready for anything too heavy. And while I couldn't see my future the way Keir sometimes could, I knew he'd always have a place in my life no matter what path our relationship took. His birth bond to me pretty much guaranteed it.

I took the grimoire from the top shelf of my closet and sat down on my bed.

Bob hopped up beside me. I petted him absently as I placed my hand on the cover over the Earth symbol. It was a ritual of mine, something I'd done multiple times.

Only now, it burned as a new surge of energy rush through me. I snatched my hand away. I watched in horror as the upside-down triangle moved to the left and on the right, a right-way up triangle appeared.

"Keir!" I was finally getting used to my new life. I had no idea what the symbol meant, but I knew it couldn't be anything good.

He burst into the room. "What is it?"

"Look." I pointed to the cover. "What in the hell is this?"

He blinked a few times then met my gaze. "It's fire." He shook his head. "But that's impossible."

I rubbed my palm. "It burned me."

Keir took my hand and turned it over. "There's no injury."

"I can still feel it." I stared at the new symbol with a

mixture of fear and awe. "I thought once an element chooses a witch, that's it. That's her one tru-craft."

He hovered his hands over the grimoire and closed his eyes. I watched his eyes twitch beneath his lids as if in REM sleep.

"What? What do you see?" His whole body was practically vibrating. I stood up and grabbed his hands. "Tell me."

"There's so many futures at once that I can't discern one from the other," he said. "But the Fire symbol appearing on the grimoire next to the Earth can only mean one thing."

"What? What does it mean?"

Keir gray eyes swirled as if in a trance. "Iris," he declared. "You've been claimed by Ignis-craft."

"No," I denied. "I'm Earth. I'm a terra-craft witch, and I'm finally starting to get decent at it."

He gazed down at me, his brow pinched with worry. "According to your grimoire, you're both."

I swallowed the lump in my throat and fought down the panic.

"Well, shit."

**The End... for now.**

**Preorder Spell On Fire (Grimoires of a Middle-aged Witch Book 2) Coming July 2021!**

## SENSE AND SCENT ABILITY

A NORA BLACK MIDLIFE PSYCHIC MYSTERY
BOOK ONE

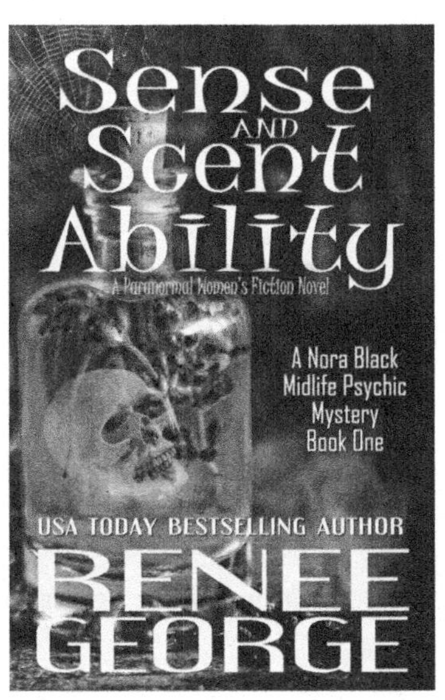


**My name is Nora Black, and I'm fifty-one years young. At least that's what I tell myself, when I'm not having hot flashes, my knees don't hurt, and I can find my reading glasses.**

I'm also the proud owner of a salon called Scents & Scentsability in the small resort town of Garden Cove, where I make a cozy living selling handmade bath and beauty products. All in all, my life is pretty good.
Except for one little glitch...

Since my recent hysterectomy, where I died on the operating table, I've been experiencing what some might call paranormal activity. No, I don't see dead people, but quite suddenly I'm triggered by scents that, in their wake, leave behind these vividly intense memories. Sometimes they're unfocused and hazy, but there's no doubt, they are very, very real.

Know what else? They're not my memories. It seems I've lost a uterus and gained a psychic gift.

When my best friend's abusive boyfriend ends up dead after a fire, and she becomes the prime suspect, I end up a babysitter to her two teenagers while she's locked up in the clink. Add to that the handsome detective determined to stand in my way, my super sniffer's newly acquired abilities and a rash of memories connected to the real criminal, and I find myself in a race to catch a killer before my best friend is tried for murder.

## Chapter One

"I think I have a brain tumor," I blurted as I flung open my front door for my best friend, Gillian "Gilly" Martin. She held a bottle of wine in one hand and a grocery bag filled with honey buns, potato chips, salted nuts, and chocolate-covered raisins in her other.

"You don't have a brain tumor." Gilly passed off the bag and the bottle, then brushed past me, shrugging off her coat and hanging it on the hall tree. It had been a cold March, with temperatures in the low 40s most days. Under the coat, Gilly wore a form-fitting, long-sleeved, baby blue turtleneck sweater and black palazzo pants that flared out over a pair of black flats. Her straight chestnut-brown hair was in a loose ponytail for our girls' night in.

"Are you pooping okay?" she asked. "The doctor said you weren't supposed to strain. You could pop internal stitches."

"Quit asking me about my bowel habits," I said. "As of yesterday, I've been cleared to resume normal activity. Like straining when I poop. Besides, I'm worried about my head, not my butt." After all, my mother had died of brain cancer. "I've been... " I trailed off, trying to find the right words. "Seeing things."

Gilly squeezed my shoulder in an effort to comfort me. "You had a hysterectomy, Nora. Didn't the doctor say you might feel strange for a while?"

Um...if strange included dying on the operating table and then discovering strong scent-induced hallucinations, then yeah. I felt strange. I mean if death was gonna bring me a gift, I would've liked something a lot more useful than the ability to smell other people's troubles.

How could I possibly explain my new weird ability to her? Well, obviously, I couldn't. It had been eight weeks since my surgery, and I still hadn't figured out a way to confide in Gilly.

"Nora?"

I sighed. "I need a drink." I lifted up the wine bottle. "Let me pop this sucker." Gilly still looked concerned, but I smiled and nodded toward the living room. "Be right there."

A few minutes later, I handed Gilly her glass of Cabernet Sauvignon and sat down next to her on the couch.

"You know, regular activities include sex," Gilly said with a little too much enthusiasm. She waggled her brows at me.

"Sex hasn't been a regular activity for me in a very long time." Two years to be exact. I wasn't a prude. It's just that there hadn't been a lot of opportunities. Between caring for my mother during the last stages of her illness and dealing with painful uterine fibroids, dating and sex were the last things I cared about.

"You are way too hot to be celibate."

"Sure." I patted my swelly-belly. "I've gained ten pounds in the last two months."

"You just had your guts cut out," she said with a fair amount of exasperation. Then she flashed me her signature Gilly Martin smile, and added, "Besides, men like women with curves."

I frowned and pinched some of my stomach fat. "It's too squishy to be a curve."

She laughed. "Girl. I got squishy curves all over." She rubbed her tummy. "Including my midsection." She fluffed her ponytail. "And I'm sexy as hell."

I grinned. "You certainly are." I had always lacked the confidence Gilly displayed about her looks and body. She wasn't wrong about her sex appeal. Men were drawn to her like bears to honey.

"Have I told you lately how happy I am that you're back in Garden Cove?"

I rolled my eyes then grinned. "All the time."

"I can't help it. I missed you when you lived in the city." Her sigh held a hint of sadness. "Though, I'm sorry for the reason you had to come home."

Last year, my mother's brain cancer had progressed to its final stage. My father had died ten years ago, and I was an only child. Mom only had me. So, I'd taken a compassionate leave of absence from work as a regional sales manager for a prominent health and beauty line to care for her. It had turned into an early retirement when my employer decided they wanted to keep my temporary replacement, a younger, more cutthroat version of myself. Thankfully, they'd offered me a generous severance package if I would go quietly, including covering medical insurance costs until I qualified for Medicare in fourteen years.

I'd accepted their offer. Spending time with Mom until her final moments had been a blessing. I didn't regret a minute of caring for her. Of course, from the hospice workers, the aides, the nurses, the volunteers who would sit with her while I shopped, and even the chaplain who brought her some spiritual comfort, I hadn't done it alone.

My mother had been the rock of our family, a major source of comfort and stability. When she got sick, she'd minimized the severity of her cancer because she hadn't wanted me to worry. Honestly, I'd believed she'd beat it. I'd never seen Mom not succeed when she put her mind to something. If only I had known how bad it really was, I would have come home sooner.

Reconnecting with Gilly had been one of the major bright spots since moving back to Garden Cove. We'd been inseparable during elementary and high school. She'd been the maid of honor at my wedding and had done the pub crawl up in the city with me when my divorce had finalized. I had been twenty-nine at the time. It was hard to believe that twenty-two years had passed since then. When I was in my teens, I couldn't wait for high school to be over so I could make my own life. Then in college, I couldn't wait to graduate so I could be married. Later, when my marriage fell apart, I couldn't wait to be out of it so I could move away from Garden Cove and start my career.

I'd spent so much time wishing my life away that I'd failed to really live in the moment. I didn't want to be that person anymore.

My whole life had been go-go-go, and I was ready for some slow-slow-slow.

I squeezed Gilly's hand. "I missed you, too. You know, it's not too late to quit your job and come work with me in the shop."

Gilly smiled. "I like running the spa at the Rose Palace Resort."

"I know you do." I didn't press her. We'd had this conversation a dozen times since I'd bought Tidwell's Diner and converted it into an apothecary, where I sold homemade beauty and aromatherapy products. I couldn't afford to pay her what she was worth, anyhow. But it didn't stop me from wishing we could spend more time together. I considered myself lucky that she'd had tonight free.

Gilly was a single mom to teenage twins, and the high school was out for their short spring break that would end on Monday and Tuesday thanks to snow days in January that they still had to make up. The kids were doing overnights at their friends, while Gilly had packed a bag to stay in my guest bedroom and leave for work in the morning from here. Hence the wine. "How are the kids doing?"

"Like they would tell me." Gilly snorted. "They're teenagers, so they share as little as possible. Marco seems to be doing okay. He's dating a girl a year older than him. A senior. Can you believe it? I wouldn't have ever dated a younger boy in high school."

"Marco's a good-looking kid."

"He's only sixteen and just like his dad," Gilly agreed. "Oozing charm and confidence. Worries me sometimes."

"He's not anything like Gio," I assured her. Marco, while moody and temperamental at times, had a kind heart, unlike his father, who only cared about himself. The twins never saw their dad anymore, and that was on Giovanni Rossi. After the divorce, he took a head chef position at an Italian restaurant in Vegas. He used his work as a way to avoid parental responsibility. Too often, Gilly carried that burden of guilt, as if it was her fault Gio had abandoned his kids.

"What about Ari?" I asked.

"She made the honor roll." Gilly's daughter's full name was Ariana Luna Isabelle Rossi. A beautiful name, but she preferred Ari. The girl marched to the beat of her own drum, and I loved that about her. Where her mother was hyper-feminine in both hair and clothes, Ari wore her hair like James Dean, and her outfits tended to be androgynous. "She's so smart, but I can't help but worry about her. She's so damned quiet. How in the world did I, a woman who can't shut up, raise a daughter who doesn't like to talk?"

"You got me there," I said, offering a sly smirk.

"Nora!" She smacked my arm. "You're terrible."

"Ouch." I rubbed the spot and laughed. "I really am.

Good for Ari, though," I said. "She's always been a smart cookie. And her drive and ambition to excel will take her places." I didn't have children by choice, but that hadn't stopped me from agreeing to be Marco and Ari's godmother. When I lived in the city, I'd sent the kids packages every year for birthdays and Christmas, but I hadn't spent a lot of time with them until I returned to Garden Cove. "She's going to be just fine, even if she didn't inherit her mother's gift of gab." I slung my arm around Gilly's shoulders and squeezed, careful not to jostle our wine glasses.

I caught the sweet scent of raspberries with notes of citrus and vanilla.

*Blurry shapes form...a woman stands in front of a large man who towers over her. Faces are hazy. It appears as if they're both made of colored smoke.*

*"It's over, Lloyd."*

*I recognize Gilly's voice.*

*"Don't be that way, Gilly," the man cajoles. "I didn't mean anything by it."*

*Gilly's voice chokes. "I really like you, but I can't be with someone who would say those things. Especially about my daughter. Ari is a great kid."*

*She turns away from him and he grabs her arm. Gilly gasps as he yanks her against his body.*

*"We belong together." He manacles both her wrists with his large hands. "You have to give me another chance."*

*"Get your hands off me," she says, pain evident in her shaking voice.*

*"I'll never let you go." His menacing tone chills me to the bone. "Never."*

"Hello." Gilly snapped her fingers in front of my face. "Earth to Nora."

"What?" I said, blinking at my friend.

Her brow furrowed. "Are you okay?"

"You're going to get grooves between your eyes if you don't stop worrying about me." Although, at this point, I had enough worry for the both of us." "How is it going with the new guy you're dating? Lloyd Briscoll, right?"

Gilly went pale and the wine glass in her hand trembled. I took it from her, then placed both of our glasses on the coffee table. "Gilly?"

"I'm fine," she said, her voice pitched to an unbelievably cheery tone. "Didn't you promise me a date with Mr. Darcy?"

I'd wanted to tell her about my scent-stimulated hallucinations, and maybe now was the time. This was the first...er, vision I'd had about my best friend. Still...what if I was wrong? If I really did have a brain tumor, and these experiences were a symptom of being sick, then it would be stupid to worry Gilly. Besides, if she thought I was nuts, she might decide to tie me up, throw me in the car, and take me to the nearest emergency room.

But her avoidance of my question, in addition to the vision, stirred a bad feeling in the pit of my stomach.

"Tell me what's going on," I said softly.

Gilly took a sudden interest in a loose stitch at the bottom of her sweater, tugging on it to avoid my gaze. "We broke up." She paused. "Correction. I broke up with him." Gilly pushed up the cuff of her sleeve and revealed finger-sized bruises on her wrist.

"He did this?" I asked. My stomach clenched. What I'd

glimpsed of Gilly and Lloyd's interaction had been real. Holy crap. Without thinking, I asked, "Was it something to do with Ari?"

Gilly gave me a sharp look. "How did you..." She shook her head then nodded. "I overheard him laughing with some of his buddies in the security office." Her hands were shaking now, and there was anger in her voice. "They were talking about Ari." Her eyes narrowed as her ire surfaced. "He called Ari a freak, and some other unsavory slurs that I won't repeat, because she happens to wear her hair short and the way she dresses."

I took her hand and gave it a pat. "He's an asshole."

"I marched right into that room gave him the it's-not-me-it's-definitely-you speech. He grabbed me and told me we were done when he said we were done."

"Is that after he told you he'd never let you go?"

Gilly paled. "Yes. How did you know that?"

Alarm kicked my adrenaline in. I skipped her question and went right to the important part. "That's a threat, Gilly. You need to call the police."

"And tell them what? Who's going to believe Silly Gilly over the head of security for the Rose Palace? Lloyd is an ex-cop, and he still has a lot of friends on the force."

"Yeah? Well, so do I."

"You mean your ex-husband chief of police who you haven't spoken to in ten years? That guy?" Gilly scoffed. "Shawn Rafferty didn't like me when you two were married."

Shawn and I had divorced for a myriad of reasons, but mostly because he'd changed his mind about wanting kids. I had not. When we divorced, we split everything down the middle, and since we didn't have children and we were both just starting our lives, I didn't sue for alimony. I didn't want anything tying us together anymore. Not even a last name, so I took back my maiden name. And then poof, like magic, it had been as if the five years we were married and the four years we dated never existed.

But say what you want about my ex-husband, he's a good cop. And, yeah, a good person. He and his wife had sent a lovely spray of lilies for my mom's funeral, and Shawn had even stopped in at the visitation. Our conversation, the first one we'd had since my dad had died a decade ago, had been short but not unpleasant.

"Shawn will believe you." I clasped both of her hands and looked her in the eye. "Promise me you'll call the police if that son-of-a-bitch comes within fifty feet of you again."

"We both work at the Rose Palace. Our paths are bound to cross." Gilly blew out a breath. "But I'll do my best to avoid him."

I stared at her hard, my mouth set in a grim line.

She raised her hand as if taking an oath. "And I'll call the police if he attempts to even talk to me." She pushed my shoulder lightly. "Now, come on. I didn't come over here to lament my tragic taste in men. You promised me a night of binge-watching Jane Austen movies, good wine, and all the popcorn I can eat."

My smile felt tight. Gilly was an adult, and she'd been living her life just fine for many years without me telling her what to do. "You're absolutely right. Let's fill up these wine glasses, and I'll start the popcorn. You break out the goodies." Like a weirdo, I loved mixing chocolate-covered raisins in with my salty popcorn. Yum.

Twenty minutes later, we were sitting on my comfy couch

with throw blankets over our legs, a large popcorn bowl between us and honey buns on the coffee table. Our wine glasses were full of Cabernet Sauvignon, and our undivided attention was on Mr. Darcy.

"Why can't real men be like him?" Gilly bemoaned after Darcy gave Elizabeth moon eyes.

"No, thank you," I told her. "I like the fantasy of Darcy, but he's judgy and bossy and arrogant. Give me a guy who is genuinely interested in my happiness, and not what he *thinks* will make me happy. That's the guy I'll spend the rest of my life with." Not that I thought such a man existed. I wasn't content exactly, but I was resigned to living out my life as a single woman. I glanced at Gilly. At least, I knew I'd never be alone. Not with friends like her in my life. I nudged her and smiled. "Even so, I'll happily root for Elizabeth Bennet to get her man."

"So, you are looking for a man," Gilly said triumphantly.

"You're the worst," I said.

Gilly made a kissy face in my direction. "Best Bitches Forever."

High-beam headlights glared through my living room window. I shielded my eyes and waited for them to go off. They didn't.

"Who is that?" Gilly asked. "Were you expecting anyone?"

"No. Just you." I got up and looked outside with Gilly right behind me.

"Oh. Oh, no," she hissed. "It's Lloyd."

"Go lock the front door," I said. When she didn't move, I said with more force, "Now!"

Gilly took off toward the front door, and I moved

quickly up the stairs to my bedroom, ignoring my creaky knees as I retrieved my gun case from my bedside table. My hands were trembling as I opened the case and grabbed my compact 9mm and a full clip of bullets. I loaded the gun while I returned to the front of the house.

It was dark outside. "Is he still out there?" I asked.

"Gilly!" I heard a man shout. "Gilly, come talk to me. I just want to talk. I'm sorry about earlier. I didn't mean it. I swear. I promise it won't happen again."

Gilly had her body pressed against the wall and out of sight. "I think he turned off the light so he could see inside," she said. "He won't stop calling for me."

"How did he know you were here?" An awful thought occurred to me. "The kids?"

"No," she said. "They're staying the night with friends." She shook her head. "I told him a couple of days ago that I was coming over here to celebrate your recovery." Her pitch went up a notch as tears flooded her eyes. "I'm so stupid."

"He's stupid. Not you."

"Gilly!" he bellowed. "Come out and talk to me. Don't make me come in there after you."

"That is just about enough." I loaded a round into the chamber of my pistol and stalked to the door. "Call the police," I said.

"I already did," she said. "What are you going to do?"

"I'm going to get that jerk off my property."

I unlocked and opened the front door, walking out with my weapon extended in front of me. The wind whipped my hair across my face, and I pushed it back with my free hand. I hadn't bothered to put on shoes, and the rough concrete from my walk bit into my socked feet. I ignored the discomfort as I took aim at the drunk in my driveway.

Lloyd, a tall man, handsome, even with a receding hairline, gave me a look of sheer incredulity. He wore a dark nylon jacket with a tear in the pocket, his cheek was red and swollen, and his lip was bleeding. I guessed this wasn't the first fight he'd started tonight.

"Get back in your car and leave, Lloyd. And stay away from Gilly," I said. "The police are on their way, and if you're gone before they get here, I won't file a complaint."

"You can't shoot me." He laughed. "Castle law means I have to be in the place you live. Otherwise, you'll go to jail for assault or attempted murder."

"The way I see it, I can shoot you, then Gilly and I can drag you into the house."

He walked up to me and pressed his chest against the barrel of my gun. "Go ahead, tough girl. Shoot me."

The sour scent of beer mixed with whiskey made my stomach roil.

*I recognize his out-of-focus form before the reek of booze confirms it. "Bitch!" Lloyd yells. He grabs a red-haired woman, his hands encircling her throat. Like Lloyd, I can't make out her face, and with her knees buckled, I can't tell how tall or short she might be, but I can feel her desperation. She struggles to escape but he is too strong.*

*"Please," she whispers, barely audible. "You're...choking...me."*

*He throws her to the ground and straddles her, his thick hands squeezing her throat. But who's his victim? I'm helpless. She's dying. He's killing her.*

I snapped out of it, full of rage. I lifted the 9mm higher

and aimed at Lloyd's head. Something in my eyes must have frightened him because he took several steps back.

Sirens sang out in the distance.

"Tick-tock," I said to Lloyd. "A smart man would already be in his car."

He scowled at me. "Crazy bitch." On that note, he jumped into his vehicle, started it up, and squealed his tires as he reversed out of the driveway.

Gilly came running outside clasping a butcher knife. "Oh my gosh, Nora. You're a freaking superhero."

"When the police arrive, I'm filing a report," I said, trying not to pass out.

She whipped the knife around in the air. "But you told Lloyd—"

"Gilly, stop waving that thing before you hurt yourself."

She blushed as she dropped her arm to her side. "I forgot I was holding it. What are we going to say to the police?"

"The truth. Lloyd Briscoll is a bad guy, Gilly. Like, really bad." I shivered as pieces of the vision played in my head. "He needs to be reported. And you need to show them your bruises. I have a feeling this man isn't going to leave you alone without encouragement."

**Click Here to Keep Reading!**

## PARANORMAL MYSTERIES & ROMANCES

BY RENEE GEORGE

**Grimoires of a Middle-aged Witch**

https://www.renee-george.com/GMW

Earth Spells Are Easy

Spell On Fire

When the Spells Blows

Spell Over Troubled Water

Ghost in the Spell

**Nora Black Midlife Psychic Mysteries**

www.norablackmysteries.com

Sense & Scent Ability (Book 1)

For Whom the Smell Tolls (Book 2)

War of the Noses (Book 3)

Aroma With A View (Book 4)

**Peculiar Mysteries**

www.peculiarmysteries.com

You've Got Tail (Book 1) FREE Download

My Furry Valentine (Book 2)
Thank You For Not Shifting (Book 3)
My Hairy Halloween (Book 4)
In the Midnight Howl (Book 5)
My Peculiar Road Trip (Magic & Mayhem) (Book 6)
Furred Lines (Book7)
My Wolfy Wedding (Book 8)
Who Let The Wolves Out? (Book 9)
My Thanksgiving Faux Paw (Book 10)

**Witchin' Impossible Cozy Mysteries**

www.witchinimpossible.com
Witchin' Impossible (Book 1) FREE Download
Rogue Coven (Book 2)
Familiar Protocol (Booke 3)
Mr & Mrs. Shift (Book 4)

**Barkside of the Moon Mysteries**

www.barksideofthemoonmysteries.com
Pit Perfect Murder (Book 1) FREE Download
Murder & The Money Pit (Book 2)
The Pit List Murders (Book 3)
Pit & Miss Murder (Book 4)
The Prune Pit Murder (Book 5)
Two Pits and A Little Murder (Book 6)

**Madder Than Hell**

www.madder-than-hell.com
Gone With The Minion (Book 1)
Devil On A Hot Tin Roof (Book 2)
A Street Car Named Demonic (Book 3)

**Hex Drive**

https://www.renee-george.com/hex-drive-series
Hex Me, Baby, One More Time (Book 1)
Oops, I Hexed It Again (Book 2)
I Want Your Hex (Book 3)
Hex Me With Your Best Shot (Book 4)

**Midnight Shifters**

www.midnightshifters.com
Midnight Shift (Book 1)
The Bear Witch Project (Book 2)
A Door to Midnight (Book 3)
A Shade of Midnight (Book 4)
Midnight Before Christmas (Book 5)

## ABOUT THE AUTHOR

I am a USA Today Bestselling author who writes paranormal mysteries and romances because I love all things whodunit, Otherworldly, and weird. Also, I wish my pittie, the adorable Kona Princess Warrior, and my beagle, Josie the Incontinent Princess, could talk. Or at least be more like Scooby-Doo and help me unmask villains at the haunted house up the street.

When I'm not writing about mystery-solving were-cougars or the adventures of a hapless psychic living among shapeshifters, I am preyed upon by stray kittens who end up living in my house because I can't say no to those sweet, furry faces. (Someone stop telling them where I live!)

I live in Mid-Missouri with my family and I spend my non-writing time doing really cool stuff...like watching TV and cleaning up dog poop

**Follow Renee!**

Bookbub

Renee's Rebel Readers FB Group

Newsletter

Made in United States
North Haven, CT
10 August 2022